# HOMICIDE

# HÉRAULT

## A Hardy Durkin Travel Mystery

By Bluette Matthey

Blue Shutter Publishing

# HOMICIDE HÉRAULT

Author: Bluette Matthey

Library of Congress control number on file with publisher.

ISBN: 978-1-941611-23-4

Other books by Bluette Matthey

From the Hardy Durkin Travel Mystery Series:

**Abruzzo Intrigue**

**Black Forest Reckoning**

**Corsican Justice**

**Dalmatian Traffick**

**Engadine Aerie**

also,

**Two Murders Too Many**

## Dedication

My honest-to-goodness thanks to my husband and helpmate, who somehow manages to navigate and organize all the craziness I manufacture with the magic wand of imagination.

Toulouse

St. Guilhem-
le-Désert

Canal

Minerve

Pézenas

Sète

Béziers

Narbonne

Carcassonne

Mediterranean
Sea

Spain

⊠ - where the
bodies were
discovered

Page from
Hardy Durkin's
Diary

# Prologue

Veteran trekker Hardy Durkin leads his first bike tour group to Béziers in the South of France, during its annual grand Feria, for what is expected to be relaxing, uneventful bicycling in the Hérault region. This notion is kicked to the curb when a double cold-case with present-day repercussions is discovered on one of the group's outings. Hardy becomes embroiled in another homicide when he is present at a murder that takes place during an innocent flamenco performance that is anything but.

The bottom line: murder and intrigue follow Hardy Durkin like a shadow, even in the sunny, laid-back South of France, but this time his wheel of fortune veers uncomfortably off the rails in **Homicide Hérault**.

Chapter One

Two men glided through the Languedoc darkness following the Canal du Midi in southern France. They had come ashore in Sète where the canal flows into the Étang du Thau and snaked their way along its bank heading north. Now they were in Béziers, at midnight, where they would pick up the River Orb to their final destination, an old mas, an ancient farmhouse, in the countryside near the ancient village of Cessenon-sur-Orb.

At the Pont-Canal-de-l'Orb, where the Canal du Midi runs atop a bridge crossing the river, the men found the stone steps leading down to the Orb and headed upstream. They skirted a night club on the river's bank, staying out of the light from a gaudy neon sign. A blowsy sax rendered a melancholy Coleman Hawkins tune out over the mild May night, and the sound of laughter tinkled when the night club's door opened and stopped abruptly when it shut again. Then all was silent except for the sound of the men slapping at the ever-present mosquitos.

Kase Devine moved effortlessly in a constant dog trot along the foot path of the Orb. His compact five-foot-nine frame carried a body taut with muscles and highly trained in self-defense and evasion tactics. Dark hair, dark eyes, Kase was an American ninja who had been employed as an American journalist in Algiers until two days ago. In reality, he was a CIA operative sent, at the behest of his government, to gauge firsthand the dynamics at play in Algeria's war for independence from their French colonial masters. It was a war that would ultimately claim a million and a half Algerian lives and ten thousand French soldiers, see tens of thousands tortured, and cause the collapse of the French government.

Foreign journalists were not welcome in Algeria in 1962. The FLN, National Liberation Front, the nationalist military and political organization spearheading the revolution, had a habit of slitting the throats of anybody they did not trust or like. Journalists were at the top of both lists. As for the OAS (Organisation Armée Secrète), the renegade group of disaffected paramilitary and Pied-Noirs (European Algerians) fighting tooth and claw to keep Algeria French, killing a foreign correspondent made big waves.

The OAS didn't care how they got international attention. Their seemingly indiscriminate bombing of libraries, hospitals, police stations, and places of business made headlines and struck terror into the hearts of all Algerians. Hardly a night passed without a fête plastique, a gala of detonations with the bombs timed and placed to unhinge the populace with their random destruction. It was hell on earth.

Kase managed to survive two weeks in Algeria, and it hadn't been by soaking up rays at the beach or whiling away time in the many cafés. The FLN had attacked Pied-Noir families vacationing in Oran, leaving the beach littered with body parts and pretty much discouraging sun-bathing-as-usual. As for the cafés ... well, they were prime targets for either warring side to toss in a grenade, Molotov cocktail, or bomb, and most now remained empty and boarded up.

Sgt. Thierry DuBlanc, Kase's traveling companion, was a contact from time spent in Indo-Chine. DuBlanc had abandoned his post in Algiers to join the OAS when the Évian Accords were signed in mid-March of 1962, giving Algeria full independence from France. DuBlanc, an Algerian by birth but French to the core, felt betrayed by his country and the army and held special enmity for De Gaulle who, DuBlanc believed, had lied outright to the military stationed in Algeria about securing the country as a part of France.

After France's humiliating defeat in Indo-Chine, the army had dug into Algeria, determined to win at all costs and restore its honor. De Gaulle had taken advantage of the army's collective sensitivity and played it in his favor until he decided to give Algeria its independence. Suddenly, the army felt betrayed; it had no clothes. Many officers as well as rank and file, feeling deceived by the turn of events and embittered that they had, once again, been sold down the river, joined the radical paramilitary OAS, the Secret Army Organization which saw itself as the only salvation for a French Algeria.

Sickened by the incessant human carnage as a result of the OAS' bombing agenda, DuBlanc had done a bunk and fled Algeria, taking with him a vital piece of information. DuBlanc had been present at Rue d'Isly on 26 March, 1962, and witnessed firsthand the massacre of his fellow French citizens. Several hundred had been shot down in the street like dogs by the army as they protested the army's blockade of Bab El Oued, a mostly European quarter of Algiers, in retaliation for killings by the OAS.

The official story was that shots had first been fired at the soldiers and their response, mowing down men, women, and children with machine guns, was a justifiable action. The black truth was that De Gaulle supporters in the army had arranged for untrained Muslim troops to replace regular French army soldiers at the blockades. French soldiers, DuBlanc knew, would never have opened fire on French citizens, but Muslim Algerians had no such affinity.

Concerned, DuBlanc had mingled among the Muslim troops at the onset of the protest listening to their whispered conversations.

"They said we can open fire if we feel threatened."

"I was told we were going to kill some Christians."

"We were transferred in from the Medea to do a job."

The firing, when it began, was butchery. The civilian procession had been led by the youth of Algiers, carrying tri-color flags, followed by men, women, and children ... whole families participated. And then came the elderly, with their slow, almost-stumbling steps. All to show their pride of being a French citizen in their beloved Algeria.

Colonel Goubard was commanding officer of the 4th RT, made up mostly of Muslim riflemen, skirmishers who were illiterate and scruffy, albeit excellent fighters. The 4th had been placed to act as a dam in Rue d'Isly, against Goubard's express wishes to his superior in command, General Ailleret. Goubard knew full well how out of hand things could become with his rough troops pitted against Europeans.

Ailleret had promised Goubard the 4th RT would not be used in that capacity. But Ailleret had bypassed Goubard and instructed Battalion Chief Poupat to deploy the 4th RT to secure the downtown areas to be engaged in the demonstration.

DuBlanc needed proof of the origin of the order to deploy the 4th RT to Rue d'Isly. He stole into Poupat's office at dark thirty in the hopes that he could find the dispatch cutting Goubard out of the command loop. His efforts had been well rewarded. Not only had he found a hastily scrawled, hand-written missive instructing Poupat's strategy, but the order also clearly pointed out that French troops were not to be used in the exercise.

"Signed by Ailleret, the bastard," DuBlanc muttered under his breath, as he made multiple photographs of the order.

The French government made no effort to investigate how the massacre had come about. It stopped just short of pretending it had never happened while an outraged French Republic clamored to know how something so horrendous could take place against its own. Still, the government said nothing, and the dead were secreted away and buried without any religious ceremony, denying friends and family the solace of a dignified burial. It was an egregious affront to the people of France.

But why? What would be the point of sacrificing French men, women, and children in such a public and heinous fashion? To whose advantage? When Thierry DuBlanc looked at this question from all sides the sick truth was that French President Charles De Gaulle's government needed an excuse for an expeditious exit from the Algerian situation with or without honor, and the pictures of an Algerian street littered with the bodies of innocent, unarmed French citizens fit the bill.

For three days DuBlanc mentally played and replayed the bloodbath he'd witnessed at the post office on Rue d'Isly. The Muslim soldiers had machine-gunned people as innocent as lambs. But the grenades hadn't come from the troops, nor the rifles fired from balconies overlooking the scene. These, DuBlanc knew, had been the OAS, exterminating the populace that supported them to make a few points in the arena of international opinion.

He was done with the insurgent group, but he doubted the OAS was done with him. He knew that the OAS didn't just let soldiers desert their cause. He had known comrades who had done the same as he was doing and they'd been hunted down and killed, their desertion seen as an act of betrayal. The OAS even sent death squads onto mainland France in pursuit of deserters.

Well, let them come after him. He'd take his chances, damn them! The madness needed to end with the nefarious duplicities exposed, and he had a piece of information that could do both. The government had deceived and abandoned the French citizens in Algeria and left the military out on a limb, once again. DuBlanc knew who had given the sanction to these state-sponsored assassinations in Algiers.

He just needed to get his information to one man: Jean-Pierre Osty. If anyone in France could expose to the world how the French government had misled, deceived, and sacrificed the French citizenry it was Capitan Osty. He would splash it on the front cover of Paris Match. DuBlanc had a name and where it led; it could bring down De Gaulle's government. And he didn't give a damn about that, either.

*****

Sometime around 2:00 AM a spotlight from a rowboat midstream in the Orb cut through the night, centering on the two men floundering with fatigue on the riverbank. Even ninjas can't melt away in headlights. The first shot severed DuBlanc's spinal cord, and he collapsed in an unceremonious heap. Kase took a torso shot and was bleeding out when the death squad waded ashore and put a bullet in his head and then one in DuBlanc's.

"Put them in the ground and let's get outta here," the squad leader barked. "This place gives me the creeps, and these damn mosquitoes are a bitch."

*****

Chapter Two

The first week of August in the Hérault department of Southern France that included the town of Béziers had been unseasonably wet in 2019. It rained steadily for three consecutive days and warnings had been sounded for possible flooding. The Aude River ran through the small town of Trèbes and parts of the village had been closed due to the river overflowing its banks.

In the direction of Béziers the Orb River had risen ominously and several villages along its course suffered food damage, with some residents being evacuated as the turbulent, muddy waters threatened houses on its banks. So much rain this close to grape harvest made the area's vast number of viticulture farmers nervous. Too much water at the wrong time could ruin the grapes.

Hardy Durkin and his travel group arrived in Béziers a week after the deluge on a Sunday, ready for some biking in the lovely Languedoc countryside. The cycling group was staying at the Hotel XIX on Place Jean Jaurès, right in the middle of the newly renovated historic city center. The Hotel XIX billed itself as retro chic, with a range of rooms catering to various comfort requirements.

Hardy had arranged for the hotel to provide more than a coffee-and-croissant breakfast for the cyclists. In addition to piping hot carafes of French press and steaming milk the morning fare also included an assortment of charcuterie, cheeses, hard-boiled eggs, juices, yogurt, toast, and fresh fruits in season from the greengrocer selling his produce on the nearby promenade.

With the gorgeous South-of-France weather back after the tempest the group breakfasted in the hotel's outdoor café, facing the plaza with its park and fountains. It was the authentic atmosphere of Southern France, also called le Midi, that everyone visiting France longed to experience and rarely did.

The first breakfast on Monday morning served as a get-acquainted session, since some members of the group had arrived late the night before. The Flomeys, Geraldine and Harold, were enjoying their breakfast at a table nearest the sidewalk when Hardy appeared on the terrasse, dressed in cargo shorts and a 'Durkin Tours' tee-shirt, his sunglasses suspended from a neoprene cord around his neck. Delia Delice had just joined them with a modest breakfast and Hardy felt their gaze swivel to him as he entered.

"Mornin' all," he called out as he headed for the Jura coffee machine set up on the small bar. 'Only the best,' he thought as he imagined Roger Federer, ambassador for Jura, smilingly handing him a perfect latte. He took note of a lynx-like cat partially hidden behind the wall of asparagus fern in a large planter just inside the wall separating the terrasse from the sidewalk. He paused to say 'hello' and the cat's tail drummed a warning. He stacked his plate with lots of protein and several croissants before joining the others.

"Not a lot of food for a day of bicycling," he commented to Delia as he dug into his assorted cured meats and eggs.

She looked from her plate to his. "I guess you're right about that," she said. "What are all those meats you've got?"

"Just the standard charcuterie medley. Ham, smoked salami, mortadella," he said, pointing to the meats as he named them.

"Morta what? Doesn't 'mort' mean dead? Is the meat something like roadkill?"

The Flomey's looked somewhat horrified at the thought, but Hardy just laughed. "Not at all, Delia. In this case the morta refers to finely ground pork ---think mortar, like mortar and pestle---- and it has pistachio added to it. Very tasty, actually."

"Oh, well, in that case I'll try some." She paused to do a wide-eyed look, then headed over to the buffet table.

Pealing laughter announced the arrival of Lilith Parasold, the newly divorced, just-turned-forty  editor of an online newspaper in Woodstock, Vermont. Hardy thought she looked like a man eater.

"You think I'm kidding, but I'm not," Fred Wannemaker was saying, looking a bit red-faced and flustered as he entered behind Lilith. His face grew even redder when he noticed he was the center of attention.

There was an awkward pause, then Lilith explained, "Fred was just telling me about the adult coloring books he designs. I'd never heard of adult coloring books, and I asked him if they were soft porn." She said this last in an off-hand manner and Geraldine jumped to Fred's defense.

"Why ever would you assume that?" she asked Lilith. "Fred is a very successful coloring book artist. His designs are extraordinarily intricate and beautiful." To Fred she said, "I especially love your collection of Old-World cathedrals and the stained-glass windows they feature."

The look on Fred's face turned from embarrassment to one of pleasant surprise. He looked older than his late 40's, due mainly to his graying brown hair, wispy matching mustache and a thin, old-man's physique with a slight stoop made by spending hours at a time bent over his drafting table.

"Yes," agreed her husband. "Your eye for detail is amazing!"

"You know his work?" Lilith asked, surprised. She just couldn't get over the concept of coloring books for adults.

"My dear," replied Geraldine, "what else can one do on those long winter nights in the Northeast Kingdom?"

"Coloring books and jigsaw puzzles," agreed her husband, nodding.

"Huh," was all Lilith could say.

"Did I hear someone mention the Northeast Kingdom?" Clive Beanstreet asked as he sidled up to the buffet table. Clive 'Call me Beany' Beanstreet owned a small group of wine and cheese shops in New England. In his early 50's, he was very proper looking, fit, and looked a bit dandy-ish in his expensively styled play clothes. No one called him Beany.

"That'd be us," Harold Flomey said, by way of introduction. "We're Geraldine and Harold Flomey." He was a warm, jolly headmaster of a small private school in St. Johnsbury, Vermont which he ruled benevolently. His wife, the vice principal, not so much. She always assumed the role of bad cop when it came to school discipline.

"Northeast Kingdom?" Delia said. "Sounds like something out of Tolkien."

"Almost as many moose as people," Geraldine said.

"I know it well," Clive said. "How did you end up on a bike tour in the South of France?"

"We were run out of Vermont by a cold, rainy early summer which resulted in a late black-fly season," Harold explained. "Nasty buggers!"

"Eat you alive," Clive agreed.

The entrance of Fania Drapeau cut the conversation short. All eyes fixed on the flamenco dancer's lithe, elegant body, her Modigliani-esque long, slender neck with her luscious black hair fastened in a knot at the nape. Her dark, flashing eyes missed nothing as they swept the terrasse, making sure she commanded everyone's attention.

Suddenly, she gave a large, open smile and glissando-ed over to the coffee bar, moving gracefully and rhythmically. Everything Fania did was dramatic. She wasn't part of Hardy's group but was staying at the hotel in preparation for the Feria, due to start the following week.

The Feria, an annual festival, attracted about a million people to Béziers for its bullfights, street concerts, and flamenco performances. Although the fête itself ran for four or five days the out-of-town street vendors moved in en masse, taking over the entire promenade of Allées Paul Riquet with their food booths and souvenir hawkers. It was one big street party the local businesses counted on to flood their coffers with tourist euros.

Instinctively, she singled Hardy out. "You are the American bicycle group, yes?" she asked.

"Yes, that's right," Hardy replied, rising from his seat and extending his hand. "Hardy Durkin," he said, introducing himself.

Eyeing his 'Durkin Tours' tee-shirt she said, "Ah, you must be the leader. Will you be in Béziers for the Feria?"

"We will," he said, "although we'll be biking around the countryside most days."

"Well, in any case, you must come to see me dance in the Parc des Poètes on Monday night, a week from today." Her voice rose perceptibly as she swiveled her graceful neck to include the entire group in her invitation. "Have you seen flamenco before?"

"Once, in Barcelona, at The Palau de la Música," Hardy said. "Impressive."

"A lovely venue," Fania said, "but formal. I think you will enjoy the amphitheater in the park. At night, under the stars … it is magical."

*****

Their first morning, after breakfast, Hardy had done his customary housekeeping session before heading out for their day's excursion. Everyone in the group had received a checklist of things to bring weeks before the trip, but experience had taught Hardy not to assume everybody had what they needed for the tour.

"The bikes were all checked again, last night, to make sure the tires were properly inflated. I'll be carrying a basic kit for repairs but anything major, like a busted wheel, is beyond my ken so just try to miss all the potholes and small children."

"Do lots of kids get hit by bikes here, Hardy?" someone asked. It was Lane Batey, the x-ray technician from New Hampshire. No sense of humor. No imagination.

Hardy refrained from a glib reply; it would only confuse Lane. "No, Lane," he said. "It was just my lame attempt at humor. Too early in the day, I expect."

Delia Delice, the forty-something red head from upstate New York did one of her wide-eyed looks with her brilliant green eyes, then went back to her normally vacuous state. She noted the gray hair tufting from Lane's ears and grimaced. 'Gross,' she thought and involuntarily moved her arm away from where it rested on the table near his cup of coffee.

"You're all pretty fit," Hardy began, "but the sun beating down on you, especially when the humidity is up, can take a toll. Just pack several bottles of water in your panniers and stay well hydrated. Oh, and grab an extra pain chocolate and a banana to keep your energy levels stable."

"Is there someplace nearby I can buy a pair of sunglasses, Hardy?"

"You're in luck, Lilith," Hardy replied. "Just up Allées Paul Riquet there are at least three optometrists, and they all sell sunglasses."

"Where's this?" Lilith asked.

Hardy pointed, "Head for that statue, hang a left, and the stores will be up on your left when you get to the theater." His look asked if she understood, and she nodded. "They won't be cheap," he added as a caution.

"Hey, not a problem," she said off-handedly. Lilith's designer clothes and accessories confirmed this.

'High maintenance,' Hardy thought.

"What's the statue, Hardy?" Geraldine Flomey asked.

"Pierre-Paul Riquet. He's the local who imagined, designed, paid for, and built the Canal du Midi. The canal's purpose was to connect the Atlantic, near Bordeaux, with the Mediterranean so France wouldn't have to ship goods around Gibraltar and pay Spain taxes to do so. Also, the canal did not have pirates, as in Barbary. It was much faster to use the 'Canal des Deux Mers', the Canal of Two Seas. Riquet is a native son and national hero," he added.

He addressed the group, "If anyone needs to buy anything else there are stores on the promenade as well as the requisite cafés and restaurants, and an amazing boulangerie just around the corner past Le Crystal restaurant. If you take this little street that runs in front of the post office, it leads to a warren of narrow walking streets filled with boutiques and specialty shops."

"What's that guy's deal?" Harold Flomey asked, pointing to one of the benches in front of the post office.

Seven heads swiveled in the direction Harold was pointing. Sitting on a bench was an elderly, heavyset man with an empty box balanced on his closely shaved head. He was engaged in   conversation with two other men who seemed oblivious of the box.

Seven heads swiveled back, waiting for an explanation from Hardy. He just smiled and shook his head. "Absolutely no idea. I think you'll find that Béziers has its requisite number of unusual characters."

*****

# Chapter Three

Bike paths on the Canal du Midi had provided entertainment for several days, but the canal was crowded and some bikers riding the canal were reckless and shouldn't have been rented anything with wheels, so Hardy had decided to bike further afield.

Hardy's group was composed of veteran travelers, and he frequently had repeat customers for Durkin Tours. Hardy's trek company catered mostly to successful businesspeople and mid-level management types who wanted to get away from their daily grind, enjoy a challenge in the wild, eat well, and sleep in a clean, comfy bed at night.

Normally, Hardy did treks to off-the-beaten path places in Europe. Last winter he had helped a friend launch her cross-country ski business in the Engadine Valley in Switzerland, rubbing shoulders with the posh St. Moritz crowd. This bike tour was a first for Hardy, and he had a few qualms about how things would turn out. More things could go wrong with a bicycle and its many parts than with human feet.

This Friday morning Hardy was taking his group through the countryside north of Béziers, with a planned stop to swim in the Orb River at a spot called Réals, located about 3.5 kilometers due west of Murviel-les-Béziers where an old, one-lane bridge crossed the Orb.

"How much further, Hardy?" puffed Lane Batey, the 53-year-old x-ray technician from Dartmouth. Lane was a bit overweight and not really in shape to do the bike tour, but he'd insisted he could keep up. Hardy had made him take a special physical administered by Lane's physician to make sure he was in good health, and he had relented when Lane passed the test.

"Not far, Lane," he replied. "The bridge is just ahead. Across the bridge and to the left."

Mentally, Lane heaved a sigh of relief. His balding pate glistened with sweat and the fringe of graying hair was moist from his exertion.

Once over the bridge Hardy hung a left and about fifty yards down a narrow, poorly paved road he pulled off to the left side under the shade of trees over-hanging the river's bank. He parked his aluminum-framed Giant Touring bike well off the road and locked it before turning his attention to his group.

Lilith Parasold, the new divorcée from Woodstock, Vermont gaped. 'Look at him,' she drooled to herself. 'What a hunk! I mean, he's gorgeous!'

Hardy Durkin was a hunk. All 6'4" of him, from his thick chestnut-brown hair to his long, tanned, muscular legs. His strong chin, chiseled mouth, not too-prominent nose (broken in a swim meet at age twelve), and intelligent, assessing deep-blue eyes were arresting in their honesty. It was a handsomely proportioned face that exuded the strength of command; he was a born leader.

Hardy had started out as a computer geek in a cubicle working for a company specializing in GPS applications in New Hampshire after active duty with the Army's SIGINT brigade in Germany. Early on he decided there was far more to life than working in a rabbit-warren office environment. During his last year of Reserve Duty, at the age of 28, he had created a nice niche business of catering to the adventurous spirit who craved quiet solitude with nature while hiking, but at night wanted a hot shower, soft bed, and the kiss of civilization nearby. Now 30, Hardy had made a success of Durkin Tours and his life, if one measured success by happiness and self-satisfaction.

More than just a pretty face, Hardy was a crack marksman and fluent in four languages. He also excelled in the pentathlon and had placed in the top five for marksmanship and swimming at the International Military Pentathlon, Military World Games, and had been a natural at signal's intelligence with the 66th Military Intelligence Brigade stationed in Wiesbaden, Germany.

He picked up on the vibe from Lilith and groaned, inwardly. The last thing he needed on one of his tours was a middle-aged single woman with her hormones out of control making passes at him. His eyes shielded by sunglasses, he glanced over his group to make sure everyone was present and accounted for.

Lane was leaning against a boulder trying to look like he wasn't on the verge of collapse. Everybody else had removed the lunch and bottled water the hotel had packed for them from their panniers and looked to Hardy to tell them where to go.

The Orb River murmured close by as it made its way to the Mediterranean Sea by way of Béziers. The river had cleared of sediment after the recent flooding and the cyclists looked forward to its refreshing water after a hot bike ride. Several paths wended the short distance to the water's edge. Hardy led his group through the trees and sparse brush as the rocky path dipped down to the gurgling river.

"No changing room?" Delia Delice pouted.

Clive Beanstreet, the wine and cheese purveyor from New England, barely stifled a snort of derision.

Hardy nodded in the direction of a cluster of trees nearby. "You'll have to make do with that one," he said. "We promise not to peek." He gave her a wink and she smiled in return.

Lilith had draped herself over a large boulder protruding into the flow, while Fred waded into the river, placing his feet securely on the rocky bottom.

"Geez, this water is cold!" he said through chattering teeth.

"It comes out of the mountains," Hardy explained. "The clarity of the water means it's probably a spring-fed river so, yes, it will be a bit nip ..."

A piercing scream cut Hardy short. All eyes turned to the copse of trees where Delia had gone to change. Suddenly, she burst out of the trees trying to run but slipping and losing her balance as she floundered toward them. The terror in her contorted face sent Hardy running to her side.

Delia latched onto him with grasping claws, her mouth moving but no sound coming out.

"Delia," Hardy said, taking her by the arms and giving her a shake. "What the hell's going on? Did you see a snake?"

She shook her head. "Nooo … no snake. Dead men," she stammered.

"What! Where?" Hardy demanded.

Delia was shivering. Geraldine Flomey arrived to see what was wrong and Hardy pushed Delia at her. "I think she's going into shock," he said.

He headed into the stand of trees. The dappled sunlight cast shadows under the boughs, but there was no mistaking what lay in somewhat of a heap in the exposed roots of the trees partially covered by river detritus brought on by the flood.

Not one, but two skeletons, one minus the skull and somewhat the worse for wear. The remaining skull's mandible was partially detached and there was what looked like a bullet hole from the forehead through to the occipital area. 'An execution,' he thought.

Hardy was not panicked by what he saw. He'd seen far worse. The past several years had introduced Hardy to death in different venues, including a grisly family murder featuring horrendous torture in Corsica.

Methodically, he studied the jumble of bones before him. Bits of tattered, rotted fabric clung to the clavicle and ribs. The frayed cuff from a sleeve bizarrely circled the bones of one wrist.

'Not much here,' he thought. Just then he caught sight of a few links from a chain that disappeared into a cluster of mud, leaves and whatever rubble the river had thrown into the mix. He gently tugged at the chain and the end came free, though it was entangled around several ribs. What he held in his hands startled him: dog tags. He was poking the remains of a murdered soldier!

He rubbed the metal tags between his thumb and forefinger to remove the mud, but the result was still unreadable. He fetched his water bottle and washed the tags so he could read them.

"'DEVINE, KASE S, 0526933, T-57 A P' … which translated to: US Army soldier Kase S Devine, last tetanus shot 1957, Blood Type A, Protestant.

"What the hell," Hardy said, half to himself, "is a US soldier's remains doing washed up on a riverbank in the South of France?"

By this time his cycling group had moved in to see what had upset Delia.

"Did I hear you say it's a dead American soldier, Hardy?" Harold Flomey asked.

"Looks like it, Harold."

"Good Lord!" Clive huffed.

"What about the other one?" Lilith asked, pointing to the other tangle of bones nearby.

Hardy turned his attention to the skeleton's travelling companion. A small oval-shaped disc with a serrated line through the middle was attached to a silver chain entangled in the rib cage. Hardy recognized it as a French dog tag. And there was something else: a small, narrow cylinder ---brass, it looked like---the size of a pencil stub, was also on the chain.

"This one was in the French army," Hardy informed them. He untangled the chain from the ribs and lifted it from the neck bone. He washed the brass container in water and dried it on the  bandana he wore tied around his neck. The brass was only starting to dezincify.

When he tried to unscrew the container, it slipped in his fingers. He used his bandana to get a better grip and tried again. Aside from a slight grittiness as he turned the top, the lid came off easily. Hardy turned the cannister upside down, but nothing came out. Odd that someone would go to such lengths for nothing. He dried his index finger on the bandana, reached in the cylinder, and extracted a small length of film.

"What the …" Fred started.

The group pressed in closer, now a single unit holding its breath. Hardy unfurled the film strip. Holding it toward the light, Hardy could make out pictures of documents of some sort but he couldn't read their contents.

"Well, what is it?" Delia demanded.

"Looks like film of some sort," Harold said.

"Film?" Geraldine quizzed. "Film of what?"

"Whatever is on that film you're holding, Hardy," Lane said, "must be pretty darn important if two men died for it."

"Were killed for it," Clive corrected.

Hardy sat back on his heels and nodded. "I agree, Lane, if in fact this is why they were murdered."

"What are you going to do, Hardy?" Clive asked.

He thought a moment, then pulled out his cell phone and checked to see if he had coverage. He speed-dialed a number.

"Clotiers," the person on the other end of the conversation snapped.

"Alain, it's Hardy."

"Hardy, mon ami!" The smile in his greeting was unmistakable. "How are you? Where are you?"

"I'm on a riverbank just over fifteen kilometers from Béziers, France, Alain. And I'm standing over the remains of two dead soldiers, one American and one, French. Both murdered in the late fifties, early sixties, if you can go by the date on the dog tags. The French soldier was wearing a small brass cannister around his neck that contains a short strip of film. Looks like pictures of documents of some sort."

There was a brief pause while Alain Clotiers processed the information. Then, "Buvain is visiting his ex-wife in Carcassonne, Hardy. Give me your GPS coordinates and he'll be there in a little over an hour."

"The police, Alain? Shouldn't they be notified?"

"Not yet, mon ami. Do nothing until Buvain gets there. Go swimming, lay in the sun, but wait for Buvain. Got it?"

"Yes, Alain."

"Depending on what Buvain reports, I'll be in Béziers tomorrow morning. It's the soonest I can get free. Say nothing to no one."

"What about my bike group?"

Alain moaned. "You've got a tour group with you?"

"Correct."

"Can you keep them quiet about this?"

"I can try." Hardy paused. "What's going on, Alain? Do you know something about all this?"

"Just a theory, Hardy," he answered. "I'll know more after talking to Buvain. Until tomorrow," and he rang off."

Hardy took a moment to collect his thoughts, then rose and turned to face his group.

"Who was that?" Fred wanted to know. "The police?"

"No, not the police," Hardy replied, shaking his head.

"Who, then?" Clive asked.

"A friend, Alain Clotiers."

"A friend," Geraldine repeated. "Why would you call a friend for something like this? Two people have been murdered; this is a matter for the police," she insisted.

Heads started to nod in agreement.

"Alain Clotiers is a special kind of friend," Hardy explained. "He's Lieutenant-Colonel Alain Clotiers, regimental commander of the French Foreign Legion 2nd Foreign Parachute Regiment stationed in Corsica. He's also the head of a Mediterranean Task Force for organized crime."

'And one of the finest men I know,' Hardy thought. His history with Alain Clotiers flashed briefly through his thoughts, beginning when they'd first met while Hardy was exploring Corsica, and at the same time trying to find out why his father had died there almost seven years ago.

Alain had enlisted Ed Durkin, Hardy's father and an old friend, to assist him on his task force tracking crime in the Mediterranean. Ed's untimely death in a car accident in Corsica had sent Clotiers into a depression of guilt for his friend's death, and when Hardy showed up on the island five years later looking for reasons for his dad's death Alain and Hardy had connected.

Hardy had solved the mystery of his father's death, discovering that he had, in fact, been murdered by a local corrupt official. In the brief course of a week on his Corsican holiday, Hardy had been kidnapped and escaped, saved Clotiers from a Russian gangster's bullet, brought his father's killer to justice, and narrowly survived an attempt on his life. The result was that in Clotiers he had a friend for life and a man who was like a second father to him.

"OK," Fred said. "So, what does the Lieutenant-Colonel think we should do?"

"He said do nothing until Captain Buvain arrives from Carcassonne."

"Who the hell is Captain Buvain?" Clive asked, exasperation starting to surface.

"Buvain is Clotiers' right-hand man," Hardy explained.

"Do you know this Buvain?" Harold pressed.

"Yes, I know him well." An image of Hardy and Clotiers storming a monk's cell in a remote Montenegrin monastery to rescue Buvain from his Roma thug captors flashed before him. Yes, he knew Captain Luc Buvain. The captain owed Hardy his life.

There was a brief lull in the questions, then Delia asked what everyone else was thinking. "Who are you, Hardy Durkin? You've got this Clotiers guy on speed dial. You're not in the least bit flustered about finding two dead soldiers on a god-forsaken riverbank in the South of France, you seem to be evading the police about it… Just who the hell are you?"

A shocked silence was interrupted by Clive. "I can answer that," he said. He turned to Hardy almost apologetically. "My cousin was on your trek in the Black Forest." To his fellow cyclists he explained, "Hardy is exactly who he seems to be. He has a trek business for points in Europe." He paused, then added, "He also has an unusual skill set from his military training and for reasons unknown to anyone has a knack for wading into mysteries, stumbling upon dead bodies, and bringing criminals to justice."

******

Chapter Four

Hardy's bike group divorced itself from the grisly remains and spent the next hour enjoying the River Orb. Lane busied himself skipping stones, a practice he'd almost elevated to the status of a hobby. The women found sunny perches on rocks overhanging the river, and the men braved the chilly water, immersing in various stages and by degrees.

Hardy eventually migrated toward where they'd left the bikes along the road, waiting for Buvain to show and when, at last, the sound of an approaching car was heard the group gravitated there, as well.

The figure that stepped out of an American Jeep Cherokee was a bear of a man. Hardy stepped up with his right hand extended in greeting, but Buvain brushed it aside and crushed Hardy to him in an embrace that would have frightened most men. When he released Hardy, he stepped back and gave him a lopsided, toothy grin that split his boulder-like face.

"Hardy, mon ami, you are looking good, if a little thin," Buvain said.

"Everyone looks thin to you, Luc," Hardy replied, smiling. The circumference of Buvain's wrist was larger than most men's biceps. Five-foot-ten and stocky, Buvain had a neck like a bull and a disposition like a pit bull. He oozed raw intelligence, which had stood him in good stead in his intelligence-gathering roles and small-team mobility missions. Buvain specialized in small weapons, including martial arts weaponry, and was a fifth-degree Tae Kwon Do black belt. He excelled at Brazilian jiu-jitsu and preferred a good old-fashioned street fight to relieve stress. He was the epitome of what a warrior should be.

Captain Luc Buvain was in his tenth year serving with Alain Clotiers in Corsica. Unlike Clotiers, who had attended École Spéciale Militaire de Saint-Cyr, Buvain had come up through the ranks in the French Foreign Legion. Clotiers had recognized Buvain's qualities of loyalty, leadership, and sense of responsibility for men under his command when Buvain led an exfiltration team in Kuwait during Opération Daguet (Desert Storm) tasked with rescuing personnel left behind in the French ambassador's residence in Kuwait after being overrun by Iraqi forces.

After Kuwait, Clotiers had Buvain re-assigned to his company back in Corsica and the two men had formed an intimate, abiding friendship over the years that transcended any difference between the two men in social status and rank.

"Harold Flomey," Harold said, stepping forward to introduce himself to Buvain with his hand outstretched.

If Buvain was taken aback he didn't let it show, but he was suddenly aware of the group of cyclists around him.

"Luc Buvain," he replied, as Harold's hand disappeared in his enormous paw.

Pulling Hardy aside he asked, "Is your group on board with the program, Hardy?"

"Not sure, Luc," he said through pursed lips. "What, exactly, is the program?"

"Let's see what you've found, and I'll let you know."

Hardy led the way to the small copse of trees sheltering the skeletal remains. Luc took it all in at a glance and knelt to examine the dog tags. The small brass cylinder he removed and pocketed, then rose to his feet. He turned to face the group.

"You're all wondering why I'm here and not the police," he began. Heads nodded around him. "It's probable that these two soldiers were assassinated carrying valuable military information."

"Is that what's in the cannister you took?" Fred asked.

Buvain zeroed in on Fred. "It would appear so."

"But this all seems to have happened decades ago," Lane said. "How could it still be relevant?"

"Military information about what? Who?" Lilith demanded.

"The late fifties and later were when the Algerians were fighting for their independence," Harold said. "Does this have something to do with that war?"

"You people ask lots of questions," Buvain said. "All I can tell you is that what you've found here could be a major piece to an historical puzzle that occurred during the time frame Harold, here, mentioned, and it is still a classified situation. The police will be notified, but military aspects of this case dictate me as a first response."

"Will the police want to question all of us?" Geraldine wanted to know.

"I'm sure they would, if they knew you were involved," Buvain answered, "but they're not going to know. I will be the only contact they have for the discovery."

"What?"

"Why!"

The group of seven's voices rose in surprise and protest. Buvain threw an inquisitive look at Hardy, who stepped into the fray.

"Captain Buvain is right about being the sole liaison with the police. The last thing we want is to get bogged down in the bureaucracy of the French gendarmes. It would be the end of the cycling trip for all of us. Luc is French; he'll know how to deal with it. Let's leave it at that."

His words had somewhat of a calming effect on his group, but he could tell not everyone was convinced. Delia had done one of her wide-eyed numbers and gone dark. Lilith and Geraldine's women's intuition reflex antennae were unsettled. The men looked like they wanted to get in a huddle and discuss the situation, but they didn't. Hardy knew he had not heard the last of this, by a long shot.

*****

"It is confirmed that DuBlanc was stationed in Algeria and joined the OAS after De Gaulle's concessions to the FLN," Clotiers informed Buvain. "As to the status of the American, I am waiting to hear back from my contact at Langley. You informed the police, Buvain?"

"Yes, mon Colonel. The Police Municipale. They'll fumble around for a day or so before calling in the gendarmes. It buys us time."

"Excellent, Buvain. Time is what we need."

"And the film, mon Colonel?"

"Were you able to read anything on it, Buvain?"

"I've handled it very little for fear of it splintering. I thought it best to wait for you to examine it," he replied.

Clotiers nodded into the phone. "I've located a microfilm reader at the Médiathèque in Béziers. We'll be able to view the film and print out a copy of the document."

"Will that be secure, mon Colonel, using the public library?"

"Tsk, tsk, Buvain," Clotiers replied. "We're not going to storm the media center dressed in our Foreign Legion fatigues. We'll just be two citizens visiting a library for research purposes. Now, where are we staying in Béziers?"

"I booked two rooms at the Hotel Mercure near the center of town," Buvain replied. "You can pretty much walk everywhere you need to go from there."

"You've done well, Buvain." Clotiers said. "I'll see you at the hotel late tomorrow morning. Where is our young friend staying with his tour group?"

"In a boutique hotel five minutes' walk from the Mercure."

Clotiers smiled. Hardy's tours did not rough it when it came to food and accommodations.

"Perfect, Buvain. See you tomorrow."

"Mon Colonel."

*****

Chapter Five

Gilles Fouque's vineyards lay on a coteaux; the hills they covered faced the Mediterranean where the grapes were kissed by the sun and nurtured by the limestone soils which had invited the Greeks to plant with vines almost twenty-five hundred years earlier.

Much had changed since the early settlers' viticulture. Beginning in the 4th century the Languedoc region became known for good wine, so much so that in the 14th century hospitals in Paris prescribed the area's St. Chinian wines for their healing powers.

Late in the 19th century that all changed with the industrial revolution when cheap red wine was produced en masse to slake the thirst of the worker bees and, later, the French soldiers who were given their daily ration. The thin Languedoc wines were combined with Algerian reds to give more body to the brew, but once Algeria gained its independence from France this arrangement stopped.

The 1970's saw the French consumer shifting to better-quality wines with the wine growers using higher-quality grapes and applying for and achieving AOC status for the wines grown in the various terroirs. AOC, or Appellation d'Origine Contrôlée, is a French certification designating a geographical region for an agricultural product: in this case, wine. The AOC designates how the grapes are grown and what wine varieties end up in the bottle.

Gilles' vines were part of the Saint Chinian AOC, an appellation known as a strong, red, tannic wine. His father, Gaspard Fouque, had fled Algeria during the Algerian revolution and settled in the Languedoc-Roussillon. Gaspard was one of the eight hundred thousand French nationals, Pied-Noirs, evacuated to the mainland in 1962 after Algeria attained independence.

In the Languedoc Gaspard did what he had done so well in Algeria: he went into viticulture. A skilled wine maker, Gaspard experimented with his wine blends, developing a less tannic, full-flavored wine with a delicate taste, as opposed to the more common strong reds that were a holdover from the days of cheap plonk.

Gilles had inherited not only his father's vines, but also his finesse and competence at blending the Black Grenache, Mourvèdre, Syrah, and Black Cinsault grapes he raised in the limestone soil. And there was another thing Gilles got from old Gaspard: his appreciation of history.

As far back as Gilles could remember his father had impressed on him the wrong done to the Pied-Noirs by De Gaulle and the bloodthirsty brutishness of the Algerian rebels. He vividly recalled visitors at their farmhouse drinking into the night with his father, all of them denouncing the French government's betrayal of the French in Algeria and the treacherous abandonment of the loyal Harkis, those Algerians who had served with the French troops in Algeria, to their brutal fate, post-revolution. Thousands of Harkis had managed to flee to mainland France; those who remained behind were summarily captured, horribly tortured, and killed. It was a chapter of French history tarred with shame.

Stories were told on those nights of the legendary OAS heroically trying to stem the tide of Algerian independence. These narrations were interspersed with incidents of treachery and butchery carried out by the FLN. To a young boy, listening in secret from the stairwell, the horrors he heard about were larger than life, impossible to conceive. The images evoked by the stories haunted his dreams and shredded his imagination.

His father had been dead for fifteen years, and many of his contemporaries were gone, as well. However, there still existed a network of the disenfranchised Pied-Noir offspring and offspring of the feared OAS in the Languedoc. It wasn't like the KKK with secret meetings or anything, but they all knew each other by name and the legacy their parents had left behind.

Still, it was a bit of a surprise when Henri Lecais, the mayor of Cessenon-sor-Orb and son of a former OAS member, stopped by unannounced on Saturday morning with something obviously on his mind. Their handshake had been brief; Gilles had returned to inspecting his grapes.

"You hear about the bodies found yesterday near the river?" Henri asked, coming straight to the point.

Gilles' head jerked back to Henri. "What bodies? Who?"

Henri glanced around to make sure they were not overheard.

"Henri," Gilles admonished him, throwing his arms wide, "We are alone. What bodies?"

"Two soldiers, one French, one an American. Shot long ago. The recent floods brought them up."

Gilles stared at Henri. "Shot how long ago, Henri?"

Lecais gave Gilles a significant look. "From the dog tags they were wearing I'm guessing the Algerian war. Both assassinated, looks like."

There was a silence while Gilles processed what he'd heard.

"Soldiers, you say? Who found them?"

"Some guy from Carcassonne fishing on the river. Went to take a piss in the trees and almost tripped over the remains." As mayor of Cessenon-sur-Orb Henri had jurisdiction over his local police and would be privileged to all information regarding the investigation. Any decisions made by the municipal police were under his direct authority.

"Gilles, this will have to be turned over to the gendarmes. I can stall reporting it to them a short while, but they will take over the investigation."

"How soon, Henri? How much time have we got?"

They both knew the implication of the discovery of the bodies. The national police would swoop down on the area asking questions and poking around indiscriminately. For people with things to hide or who had a healthy distrust of authority, the thought of gendarmes sniffing everywhere was a threat that could only lead to trouble. They also knew, even so many decades later, that the wound of the Algerian war for independence and the accompanying war crimes could still suppurate under the thin skin of the passage of time.

The OAS hadn't really gone away; it lay dormant, like a submerged swamp creature with its watchful eyes just above water level. And the Pied-Noirs, although fully integrated back into French society, would always carry the trauma of Algeria, passing it down to succeeding generations as part of their living history. It would forever be part of their gene pool.

Henri knew Gilles was involved with the JPN, the Jeune Pied-Noir, an organization of the second generation of French national refugees from Algeria after the FLN won independence from France. Outspoken and angry, the JPN never forgot or forgave the French government, and specifically De Gaulle, for selling out the Pied-Noir in Algeria and abandoning the Muslim Harkis. It was a movement fed by emotional dross.

"I can give you until tomorrow morning, then I'll have to pass it up the line."

"This fisherman that found them … do you know where he is?"

Henri nodded. "I've got his contact info. He's staying in Béziers at the Hotel Mercure on Saint- Saëns. Name's Buvain. Beefy guy, in his thirties. You ask me, he looks military."

*****

Chapter Six

Hardy made a point of being in Béziers when Alain Clotiers arrived. It was a day scheduled for the bike tour to take a day off from pedaling and catch up on laundry, local sightseeing, or just relaxing.

The members of his tour group had checked in with him, so he knew everyone's itinerary. The Flomeys and Fred were taking a walking tour around the ancient town, starting with what remained of the Roman arena.

"Béziers is the second oldest city in France, after Marseille," Harold commented. "And it has loads of quirky things to explore. For instance, just around the corner from the old amphitheater is a small plaza where Saint Aphrodise, a Christian who came from Egypt riding his camel, was beheaded."

"Eeww! For real?" Lilith asked.

Geraldine nodded. "Not only that ... he didn't die, but he picked up his head and carried it back to the cave where he was living on the other side of town. He is a cephalophore, a saint depicted carrying his own head.... Anyway, as he was walking down this little street a bunch of stone masons made fun of him and when Saint Aphrodise looked at them, they turned into stone."

Clive rolled his eyes. "It's called marketing, guys." 'Designed to suck in weak-minded believers and suckers,' he wanted to add, but didn't.

"There's a basilica built over the cave where he was living. It's quite famous, and the oldest church in Béziers."

"The Way of Saint James runs through Béziers, as well," Hardy informed them, "for any of you interested in pilgrims. Also, the Via Domitia, the ancient Roman road that connected Rome to Spain. Lots of history here, if you're interested. Plus, there's the Oppidum d'Ensérune about fifteen minutes from here. It's an archaeological dig of a Gallic settlement dating back to the 6th century BC. We could bike there one day, if you'd like."

"Oh, yes, let's!" Delia said. "I've never seen anything that old, and I can tell Raynor all about it." Raynor was Delia's wealthy real estate investor husband in upstate New York. He'd suggested the cycling tour to his wife as a means of getting her out of his hair and in the hope that it might expand her limited, self-centeredness.

"Great! We can combine that with a trip to the Écluses des Fonseranes, which is another unique attraction here, and end with a picnic there. It would be an easy day, but really interesting."

"What's the Aycloose of whatever you said?" Lane asked.

"The Écluses des Fonseranes, the nine locks built on the Canal du Midi by Pierre-Paul Riquet, the genius who designed, engineered, and paid for the Canal to be built. Remember the big statue on the promenade? The Écluse is a staircase of locks Riquet designed to overcome the difference in height between the Garonne River, at the other end of the canal near Toulouse, and the water level here. He didn't actually build the locks. The two Medailhes brothers, along with mostly women, built the locks."

"Why women?" Lane asked.

"Well, these were women from the Pyrénées Mountains, and they understood timbering and using timber gates in weirs. Peasant women had built dams for logging in the Pyrénées. It was just something they understood, had a sense of, and they built the lock staircase at Fonseranes."

Changing the subject, Hardy asked, "Lane, what are you doing today?"

"Uh, I need a few things from the drug store, and then, I dunno …."

"There are several pharmacies along the Allées Paul Riquet on the far side of the wide walking area," Hardy told him. "And today, Saturday, is brocante day on the Allées. Lots of vendors selling anything from antiques to books and music, to furniture and clothes, all second-hand. Check it out. You'll be amazed at some of the stuff for sale. Plus, it's a great place to people watch. Just beware of pickpockets; gypsies are always around."

"What kinda clothes?" Lilith wanted to know.

"Mostly vintage stuff, Lilith." Her face fell. "But these little back streets have all kinds of clothing boutiques and specialty shops. You can wander around for hours."

"How about wines and cheeses?" Clive asked.

Hardy nodded. "Follow this street, Citadel, in front of the Post Office, until you come out on another busy, larger street. There'll be a small plaza ringed by restaurants. Opposite the Hotel de Ville. And the tourist office is there, too. Head up past the tourist office and you'll come to the covered market, Les Halles. Inside the market are a few cheese and charcuterie vendors, and there are shops for wines all around the market in the surrounding streets, as well as a specialty cheese vendor."

Clive nodded his approval and appreciation.

"Right," Hardy said. "I've got an appointment to meet a friend, so I'll see you all later. I've made reservations at a typical Bitterois restaurant for this evening, Le Massilia, for eight o'clock. It's on the corner opposite Les Halles. They have a decent menu of regional dishes, if you're interested."

He glanced around the group, tallying up the nodding heads; it was unanimous.

"Good. Then I'll see you all at Le Massilia."

*****

Hardy set off for the hotel where Clotiers and Buvain were staying on Saint-Saëns. He crossed over the wide Allées Paul Riquet where the second-hand market was in full swing. Old clothing and accessories, furniture, books, CD's, comic books, and endless household items, including some fine china and lighting, were for sale by an assortment of vendors.

Shoppers ambled from display to display examining the plunder. Dogs on leashes, accompanying their masters, sniffed a world of ancient smells, no doubt wondering what it all meant and excited by the new stimuli.

In the midst of the promenade reigned Mr. Box Head, a small cardboard box balanced on his head containing assorted canned goods with a long baguette perched judiciously over the box. Mostly, people tended to ignore him, and he was impervious to the few stares that he got.

Suddenly, Mr. Box Head threw his hands out in front of his torso and launched into a soft-shoe routine. It was a bold move. The box started to slide off to the left and the dancer corrected in the nick of time, but he gnashed his teeth when the baguette fell and he was forced to catch it in his hands, giving it a filthy look at its betrayal.

'He must be a permanent fixture in Béziers, to be so ignored,' Hardy thought. For all his large size it was impressive that the old guy had such good balance.

Hardy arrived early for his meeting with Clotiers and Buvain at the Mercure next to the Palais de Congress. The breakfast room was empty, so he inquired at the desk for Clotiers room number and took the elevator up to the second floor.

As he approached the end of the hall where his friends' rooms were located, he noticed a wooly-looking, bearded man who appeared to be listening at the door to Buvain's room.

"Can I help you?" Hardy called out, still thirty feet away.

Surprised, the mystery man bolted for the entrance to the stairs and disappeared through the door. Hardy thought about giving chase, but instead knocked on Clotiers' door.

Alain opened the door, a wide smile on his face. He embraced Hardy with affection. "Mon ami, …" he began.

But Hardy interrupted. "Alain, I just surprised a guy listening at Buvain's door. He ran off when I called out to him. Beat it down the stairs."

Buvain heard this last as he moved up behind Clotiers. Alain nodded in Buvain's direction, who took off down the stairwell in pursuit.

"Buvain will sort it out."

Hardy had a brief mental visual of what the guy would look like if Buvain caught him and sorted it out. Not a pretty thought.

"Come in, mon ami," Clotiers was saying. "Coffee?"

Hardy shook his head. "No, thanks, Alain. I'm good."

They sat in the room's small lounge area. There was an awkward pause. "So," Clotiers said, "we meet again, eh, and under the usual suspicious circumstances." He pummeled Hardy's shoulder and both men laughed, the awkwardness dispelled.

Meeting under bizarre circumstances was the norm for Hardy and Clotiers. The first time had been when Hardy visited Corsica, saving Clotiers life and finding his father's killer. The second time united the two men in Montenegro with the purpose of finding and rescuing Buvain from Roma thugs and kidnappers, and now this.

"How is your mother, the lovely Lydia?"

"She's doing fine, Alain. When's the last you spoke to her?"

Clotiers colored. "I confess, too long ago. I had hoped to stop in Frankfurt a fortnight ago for a brief visit, but plans changed."

It was no secret to everyone who knew them that Hardy's mother, Lydia Durkin, and Alain were in love. No secret to everyone but Lydia and Alain. Both were so set in their ways: Alain a bachelor married to the Legion and his men, Lydia comfortable with her grandchildren, roses, and several successfully run internet cafés.

Hardy stifled a sigh. Two of his favorite people. 'You can bring a horse to water, but you can't make him drink,' he thought.

"Hardy, if you would, tell me exactly what happened when you found the remains of the two soldiers. I've heard Buvain's account, but I also need to hear your version."

Hardy recounted the events of the discovery, beginning with Delia looking for a place to change into her bathing gear and ending with his call to Clotiers after the grim discovery. Alain listened without interruption, nodding to himself during the recantation.

Buvain arrived back from his pursuit of the stranger and shook his head at Clotier's expectant look.

"Well, we know we must be vigilant," Clotiers said. "Someone is interested in us, to the point they've sent a spy." He looked pointedly at Hardy and Buvain. "Let's take our bit of film to the Médiathèque and see if we can find what has aroused this curiosity."

***** 

"This confirms rumors I'd heard about what went down that day on Rue d'Isly," a somber Clotiers said. "Even though it happened over fifty years ago it is still distressing to see proof that the rumors were true."

"So why is this relevant now, Alain?" Hardy asked.

Clotiers shrugged. "Not perhaps relevant, Hardy, but damning to the government, even now. At the time this incident took place there was such outrage that it happened and even more fury at the government's cover-up, for that is what it was. Keep in mind that the Fourth Republic had collapsed eight years before, in 1954, and the current regime was stumbling its way through the mine field of the war with Algeria. At times it seemed De Gaulle was barely holding the government together and this information would probably have toppled it."

"Yes, but as you pointed out, it was over half a century ago."

"Oui, mon ami, but there exist even today remnants of organizations that would take this confirmation of the atrocity and run with it. It would fan the flames of long-smoldering antagonism toward the powers that be."

"So, what are you going to do with this?" Hardy wanted to know.

Clotiers scrunched his shoulders several times to ease the tension and slowly rotated his head from side to side, thinking.

"For the time being, nothing. I'll wait to hear from the Americans."

*****

Karim Aboud was sitting on the wall outside Médiathèque, smoking, in a group of Arab-looking men doing what they do well: talking and gesticulating. He knew he had been lucky to have avoided capture by the massive man who pursued him after Hardy exposed his snooping. When Hardy and company exited the media center he waited until they had crossed the large plaza fronting the building and then headed off in a slow pursuit.

When Clotiers and Buvain peeled off at Hotel Mercure Karim followed to see where this third person was staying. At Hotel XIX Hardy picked up his key at the desk before heading for his room. Clive Beanstreet was in the lobby as Hardy walked past, talking on his cell phone. Hardy gave Clive a thumbs up and Clive responded with a nod and a "Hey, Hardy."

"Our tour leader just went by," Clive said into his phone. "You know, the guy who found the bodies and made the phone calls. He knows people, I'm telling you."

Karim's face remained impassive, but his eyes darted back to where Hardy was disappearing up the stairs. 'So, it was you who started the wheels in motion,' he thought. 'Just who do you know, my American friend?'

*****

## Chapter Seven

Dinner at Le Massilia that night was a festive affair. With Feria week starting in a few days there was more of a buzz everywhere and Le Massilia was no exception. The waiters all wore red berets, common head gear during Feria, and the interior of the restaurant was hung with paintings and posters of bull fights and famous matadors.

Lilith blanched at the graphic pictures of the corridas.

"Dear god, how cruel!" she exclaimed. "How can anyone watch something like this and enjoy it?"

"Lots of people love bullfights," Hardy told her. "There's a constant back and forth between those who are in favor of them and those who think they're inhumane and should be abolished."

"Don't the poor animals suffer horribly?" Geraldine asked.

"Suffice it to say, yes, they do," Hardy replied. "In Provence, however, the concept of bullfights is totally different. They don't kill the bull. The bullfight in Provence is called *la course Camarguaise*, and   the goal of the Camargue matador, or *raseteur*, is to pluck a ribbon from between the bull's horns using razor blades attached to the ends of their fingers. The bulls are never harmed, but it is very dangerous for the raseteurs. They are constantly jumping into the bleachers to escape the charging animals." He paused. "I suggest we change the subject or some of you won't want to eat your dinner."

The abrupt end of the discussion created an awkward moment, which was dispelled by the waiter zeroing in on their table to take their orders.

Lane pointed to his choice of entrée and main course, hoping for the best since he didn't read French. When Hardy explained what he'd ordered, poached egg in blue cheese cream sauce with smoked bacon and guinea fowl with citrus fruits in a currant gelée, he was delighted.

The Flomey's opted for the small salad with warm goat's cheese and entrecote with a white pepper sauce.

"Can't ever go wrong with steak frites in France," Harold said.

Clive opted for a cocotte of little sea snails with tarragon butter and veal kidney in a wine and parsley sauce, and Fred ordered pig's feet and ravioli in a white truffle sauce with basil.

Lilith and Delia both ordered prawns for their entrée. Lilith went with a hamburger à la maison, and Delia decided on the chicken burger.

"And I'll have the gambas bisque and the entrecote, à point, with frites," Hardy said.

"What's à point mean?" Harold asked.

"It's how I want my steak done …. medium rare."

"I want my steak well done," Geraldine said.

"That'd be 'bien cuit,'" Hardy told her. He signaled to the waiter and told him to prepare Geraldine's steak bien cuit.

After the food was ordered the group selected several bottles of wine from the Saint Chinian AOC. With the wine flowing, the group got chatty.

"There's an old church just up the street, Madeleine or something, with a plaque on the wall that says, "Kill them all, the Lord will know His own." What's that about, Hardy?" Fred asked.

Hardy nodded and finished swallowing his wine.

"Back in 1209 there was a religious sect, the Cathars, who had some beliefs that really flew in the face of the Catholic Church."

"Such as?" Lilith asked.

"Well, the Cathars rejected the Catholicism of Rome and believed that since there was so much evil on the earth it had been created by Satan. They believed in two gods; the good god was the god of the New Testament who was also the creator of the spiritual realm. The god of the Old Testament was evil, aka Satan. The Cathars also didn't believe in the spiritual Trinity of Father, Son, Holy Spirit. Just stuff like that that didn't sit well with Rome."

"Let me guess," Harold said. "Rome loosed the dogs on the Cathars."

"Big time," Hardy said. "It was called the Albigensian Crusade and it killed around a million people in the South of France, and not just Cathars. Lots of collateral damage."

"Who was pope then?" Lane asked.

"Innocent III, but he was not very innocent. He chose a brute name Abbot Arnaud-Amaury to head up the crusade to wipe out the Cathar sect, and the good abbot went zealously about his task. Béziers was the first Cathar stronghold attacked. The Cathars in Béziers were liked by the general population and the citizens of Béziers, population around 20,000 at the time. Béziers refused to give the Cathars up to the crusaders, so Amaury infamously told his soldiers to 'kill them all; God will know His own.' So, 20,000 men, women, and children were put to the sword and the city burned. Many took refuge in that church you mentioned and the Saint Nazaire Cathedral. Both burned, with people inside."

There was a stunned silence around the table while the horrific historical information was processed.

"My god!" Geraldine finally gasped. "A town of 20,000 people back in 1209 was a big town! All massacred!"

"Did it end here, in Béziers?" Delia asked.

Hardy shook his head. "The pope's army pursued the Cathars all over the Languedoc-Roussillon, putting them to the sword or burning them alive. As you enter the lovely village of Minerve, west of here, you'll see a monument to the 180 Cathars burned alive in Minerve. And the Cathar castles …. They'd be put under siege until the Cathars inside gave up and came out, only to be put to death when they refused to recant."

"Sounds like genocide," Fred said. "How long did this crusade go on?"

"Roughly twenty years," Hardy replied, "but the eradication lasted beyond that. It took on political aspects in redistributing the conquered land and confiscated wealth. You know how that works."

Their bereted waiter appeared, asking if dessert and coffee were desired. Crème caramel, tarte aux pommes, and ice cream were the popular choices, but Clive, ever the sophisticate, ordered the cheese plate.

"What's the latest on the dead soldiers, Hardy?" Lane wanted to know.

All eyes swiveled to the head of the table. The question appeared to have caught Hardy off guard, a rare occurrence. He glanced somewhat nervously around before answering.

"Uh, nothing new, really, Lane," he responded.

"But didn't you go see Buvain and that Clotiers fellow earlier today?" Fred pressed.

"Yes, but ..." he began, before Lilith jumped in.

"Well, didn't you guys look at that bit of film you took off the body? What was on it?"

"Just some old documents," he replied. "Nothing of current interest."

"So, have the cops been by to talk to you?" Clive wanted to know.

"Ah, no, Clive. Buvain is the go-to guy with the cops, remember?"

Clive wasn't satisfied with this answer. "Yeah, but is he telling them everything ... like the film?"

"No idea," Hardy answered, with finality.

Lilith opened her mouth as though to speak but shut it and said nothing. Message received: Hardy didn't want to discuss it further.

*****

"It's actually some Yank heading a bike tour who found the bodies yesterday," Karim told Gilles after following the group back to their hotel from Le Massilia. "It might be easier to question him than taking on a couple of muscle men."

Karim Aboud was the son of a Harki who had escaped post-independence Algeria. Gaspard Fouque had sponsored Sami Aboud and his wife to emigrate to mainland France with Gaspard's family and followed through with employing Sami in his grape-growing business. The families had remained close, even after the passing of the two patriarchs.

"Does he really know anything?" Gilles wanted to know.

"I'd say so, Gilles," Karim replied. "I overheard a member of his tour group saying the Yank was the one who called in those two staying in the Mercure."

"Interesting.... I wonder why he called them instead of the cops."

"I'm guessing he found something unusual with the bodies. One of his bike group members said something about some film he lifted off one of the dead guys. They probably went to the Médiatheque to use the microfilm reader to view the film."

"What film?" Gilles was quick to ask.

"Something about old documents and not of current interest. Look, Gilles, I think those two guys at the Mercure are army intelligence or something. They've got the look. They wear their civilian clothes like uniforms. Hell, I wouldn't be surprised if they're Legionnaires."

There was a short, stunned silence on Gilles' end of the phone. Then, "You take care, my friend. You take very good care."

*****

Chapter Eight

The next day's itinerary cycled Hardy's group to Sète, on the Mediterranean, by way of the ancient Greek town of Agde along the Canal du Midi. The day was superb. The bluest of clear skies, not too hot, with just a bit of a sea breeze to evaporate the sweat. Sète is a major port city in southern France that balances on a small isthmus of land between the Étang du Thau and the Mediterranean. It is called the 'Venice of Languedoc' because of the many canals that crisscross the town, linking the two bodies of water.

The group decided to check out Sète's indoor Sunday market at Les Halles, savoring the ambience of friends and neighbors enjoying fresh foods and good company. The market was a cacophony of smells and colors, with vendors selling the usual cheeses, charcuteries, vegetables, flowers, olives, baked goods, meats, and prepared foods. This particular market, since Sète is surrounded by water, features an abundance of sea creatures indigenous to the area, both fresh and in a variety of cooked dishes.

"Wow! The seafood is incredible!" Even though Clive was a New Englander, he was always inspired by fresh fruits de mer.

"You really need to try the black olive tapenade from that vender over there," Lilith gushed, finishing off a free sample and indicating a food stand across the aisle from where they stood.

"Let's meet back at this entrance in an hour," Hardy suggested. "That way, everybody can explore on his own. It's easier than trying to keep the group together. Just don't snack too much on the freebies; we're going to lunch on the quay when we finish here."

Lunch in Sète was a smorgasbord of freshly caught seafood, with raw oysters on the half shell from the nearby village of Bouzigues getting rave reviews. After a lazy amble along the wharf the group headed back in the direction of Béziers, stopping at one of the many beaches west of town to soak up the sun, doze off the wine from lunch, and enjoy the sea.

When they returned to their lodgings late that afternoon, weary, bloated with sun, and very satisfied on a day well spent Hardy discovered that his room had been inexpertly searched but nothing had been taken. When he mentioned this to the front desk his query was met by the bearded, dark-haired, dark-eyed clerk with a few unsympathetic clicks of his tongue and an impassive face.

*****

The tour group woke to a flurry of activity Monday morning as the wide promenade of Allées Paul Riquet, lined on each side by large, ancient plane trees, was taken over by an assortment of vendors and venues participating in the Feria, Béziers' festival featuring bull fights, equestrian events, flamenco dancing, and food, transforming the area into a carnival-like celebration.

"What in the world?" Lilith gaped as the group gathered for breakfast.

"It's the annual Feria, Lilith," Hardy replied. "Later this afternoon, they'll open the festival with a mass in the bull-fighting arena, followed by a parade through town carrying a richly jeweled statue of the Virgin, along with a band and maybe some horses and lavishly costumed riders. Then there'll be live music blasting on the Allées until 2 AM. You'll appreciate that our hotel is set back from the promenade. By tomorrow the Feria will be in full swing."

Food cabanas hawking a variety of foods from a handful of countries were prominent, with free samples being offered to passersby. The Brazilian tent was popular, with succulent slices of grilled beef being shaved off for tasting. A German tent specialized in sausage and beer, and several of the local brasseries offered their French fare. Enormous wok-like skillets of paella enticed hungry festival goers to dine, while the Turkish fast-food establishments attracted the budget-minded.

There were also small concerns selling souvenirs to remind you that you had attended the largest festival in the South of France, plying everything from mugs, flags, tee shirts, and red berets to an array of cheap, gimmicky toys for kids of all ages. Lots of balloons. It was a fair-like atmosphere with some class.

Stages had been set up at each end of the immense promenade and individual musicians and bands entertained and enlivened at set times throughout the day and evening, on into the early hours of the morning. It was a giant block party. Lots of beer, wine, smoking dope, and no violence. Just good clean fun for the whole family.

"You will, of course, come see me dance flamenco in the park tonight?" Fania Drapeau had entered with her usual graceful flourish, the long, full skirt swishing seductively around her ankles.

"Wouldn't miss it!" Fred promised.

Fania threw Fred an appreciative smile, then turned a quizzical look on Hardy.

He threw up his hands. "Of course, Fania. The whole bike group is planning on attending."

A shadow and chill moved across the terrasse when a man in his early thirties approached Fania. The scowl on his face seemed perpetual. He whispered something in the dancer's ear and waited.

Fania's immediate response appeared something akin to revulsion but was instantly over-ridden by a forced smile. She was aware of Hardy's interested gaze.

"Hardy, this is my agent, Manuel Pirón."

"Manuel, Hardy Durkin," Hardy said, his hand extended.

The manager's response was a lessened scowl accompanied by a handshake that left Hardy feeling like he had just exchanged greetings with a dry, scaling tree branch. And limp-wristed, on top of it. Manuel clicked his heels together, gave a curt nod to everyone, turned on his heel, and went back into the hotel.

'Something off about that guy,' Hardy thought. This was confirmed by an odd tingly itching in the back of his throat. Never a good sign. Señor Pirón would bear watching.

\*\*\*\*\*

## Chapter Nine

Every year around 2.5 million people worldwide are forced into some form of trafficking, either as a slave laborer, sex worker, domestic slave, victim of organ trafficking, forced begging, or some other criminal activity. Fully eighty per cent of the victims of trafficking are women and children.

Even terrorist groups have joined the ranks of human traffickers, using trafficking as an act of terror, a source for recruitment and, also, a financing strategy. There is a lot of money to be made in human trafficking, to the tune of thirty-two billion-with-a-B dollars a year. Tax free.

To a morally compromised man like Manuel Pirón, the allure of trafficking dollars was too good to pass up so, in addition to acting as agent to a dozen or so artists, he also ran a human trafficking operation from Spain into France.

Migrants fleeing African countries generally head for the northern area of Morocco for a sea departure across the Strait of Gibraltar to Algeciras, Spain. The distance between the two countries at that point is a nine-mile journey by sea.

Migrants have few choices on their sea passage: they can pay several hundred euros to cross in a small boat packed to the gun wales and susceptible to sinking, or up to five thousand euros to cross on a jet ski. Nine miles of open sea on a jet ski is a long trip which most migrants cannot afford, so they opt for the cheaper route. The hope is that the Spanish Coast Guard will pick them up sooner rather than later and transport them to a migrant reception center on Spanish soil.

Once at a center they wait for a smuggling network to get them out of the overloaded, chaotic holding camps and send them to wealthier European countries further north, like France, Germany, or the UK. Often, gangs hijack them as they travel, and migrants are ever at the mercy of the smuggling networks who exploit them as laborers or in the sex trade.

Pirón's smuggling operation picked up migrants near the French village of Cerbère on the Spanish border and transported them, usually by produce truck, to the outskirts north of Béziers. Once there, they would have a week or so to acclimate and then would be dispersed to either Toulouse or Montpellier, large cities where they can be absorbed without notice while being inducted into the vice chosen for them to earn money for their minders.

A few of the more matronly women are chosen to act as mothers to a variety of minors traveling alone, giving the appearance of a family seeking asylum and a new life. Falsified documents, a whole other lucrative illegal business, are provided as a means of insuring the children are provided for by the State while being trained and indoctrinated for future use by their owners. It is a sad and vicious life for the victims, and one the French government is determined to eradicate from its soil.

*****

France's Ministry of the Interior, which faces the Élysée Palace, is located on Place Beauvau in the Hôtel de Beauvau in the 8th arrondisement in Paris. The building houses the General Directorate for Internal Security, the DGSI, which is responsible for counterintelligence, counterterrorism, and surveillance of potentially threatening organizations, groups, and social phenomena on French territory.

After a wave of deadly terrorist attacks on French soil in 2015 the government woke up, sat up, and realized it had better ramp up its national security after budget lapses left homeland security marginally and peripherally provided for following the Cold War.

The wake-up call revealed a country at war on its own soil operating under an entirely different ethos. It was a war for which France was unprepared and it caught the nation by surprise. The tenets of this new war found France unable to protects its citizens and its territories, a realization which brutally shocked the populace.

With the new spirit of defense that resulted from these terrorist attacks, as well as a hastily increased budget, the government put thousands of troops on the streets as a show of force and gave police officers the authority to carry weapons at all times, even when off duty. Police were granted the right to search anyone using public transportation who looked suspicious, and metal detectors were installed on certain train platforms. Several thousand people were recruited to work in intelligence and surveillance, and the French Patriot Act was passed which gave the government sweeping powers to spy on its citizens. It was a new day in the Republic.

Colonel René Duclos had been part of the Gaullist paramilitary, the MPC (Mouvement pour la Communauté), formed in Algeria, initially, as a political movement. The MPC very quickly evolved into a military group nicknamed 'Le Talion' (The Retaliation) to counteract the violent OAS.

Also called 'les barbouzes', or bearded spies, these brutal irregulars passed information they picked up from locals on to the French secret service, the General Directorate for External Security, or DGSE. The OAS put a stop to this by systematically killing off most of the MPC informants in Algeria.

René Duclos had survived by being recalled to Paris before the extermination began, but he spent the rest of his life looking over his shoulder, a life cut short by an unsolved hit-and-run two blocks from where he lived in Saint-Germain-des-Prés.

His son, Claude Duclos, had picked up his father's mantle and joined the Ministry of Interior's DGSI. Claude's job was oversight of groups and individuals who posed a threat to France and its citizens. To that end, Duclos had a dedicated network of spies and informants embedded throughout France whose purpose was to listen to and engage in discourse on all levels of society, noting any revelatory tidbits that could in any way be construed as a menace to the homeland and reporting it, directly, to Duclos.

The Monday morning after the soldiers' remains had been discovered in the Hérault Duclos' phone rang. It was his colleague, General Robert Durand, from the Director-General's office of the National Gendarmerie.

"Duclos."

"Robert Durand, Claude. Something was just brought to my attention, an incident in the Hérault. It's probably nothing, but I wanted to put you in the loop, you understand." General Durand paused; Duclos waited.

"It could do with something that happened decades ago, during the Algerian war, so the chance of problems arising from it are remote."

Duclos lost his patience. "What's the situation, General?" he almost snapped. Durand just loved to hear himself talk. 'Cut to the chase, Bob," he thought.

Durand cleared his throat. "Remains of two dead soldiers found outside Béziers. One French, one American. Assassinated, looks like."

Duclos' ears pricked up. Assassinations always made for a messy business. They were never simple, in his experience.

"Do we have identification?"

"We've found the service record for ours and contacted the Pentagon about the American. Still waiting to hear back."

What makes you think it's related to Algeria?"

"The dates on their dog tags. Puts them right in the middle of it."

"Who found the remains?"

Durand paused. "That's the funny part," he said. "A Captain Luc Buvain, French Foreign Legion, stationed in Calvi."

"Why is that funny, General?"

"Captain Buvain is the right hand of Lieutenant-Colonel Alain Clotiers, also of the Legion. Buvain called in Clotiers on the find and the two men are now in Béziers. Doing what, I've no idea. But I am telling you this, Claude, if those two are investigating, they smell smoke."

*****

Duclos' initial reaction to his conversation with General Durand was to place a call to a contact in the Prefect's office in Toulouse.

"Good morning, Étienne. Claude Duclos, Interior. Who do we have in the Hérault near Béziers?"

Duclos' call caught Étienne Brélot off guard. "Ah, ah, yes, Duclos. Thierry Jean, in the Sous-Préfecture. Seems to know everybody in Béziers."

"Get a hold of him this morning, Étienne. We need eyes and ears in Béziers." Duclos explained the situation to Brélot. "Find out where the Legionnaires are staying in Béziers and put a tail on them. I want to know where they go, who they talk to…everything."

"Right away, M. Duclos."

Étienne sat a moment with the phone to his ear even after Duclos had rung off. It amazed him that after all the time that had passed since the Algerian conflict there were still people in government at the highest places exhibiting paranoia and chasing boogey men. Still, his was not to reason why. If Duclos wanted to play at shadows and espionage, so be it.

Étienne Brélot rang the Sous-Préfect's office in Béziers and was put through to Thierry Jean. "Thierry, Étienne Brélot. Good morning to you."

Thierry was instantly on his guard. Brélot came across as a hail fellow well-met when, in fact, he was a pompous man who intimidated by being overly solicitous. He came from a once well-to-do family in Toulouse and although he was no longer wealthy, he retained the arrogance of his class.

"I just had a call from Paris ... Ministry of Interior .... and I have an assignment for you from the top."

Thierry was most definitely intrigued, but at the same time smirked at Brélot's choice of words. 'Such a fool,' he thought, but he listened, intently, to Brélot's instruction.

"You think these Legionnaires are investigating what? A crime that has long gone cold? To what end, Brélot?"

"It could be a big deal, Thierry. Just do it," he huffed. "And keep me informed."

Thierry's smirk widened. Indeed, Étienne Brélot didn't have the ability to think outside the box and he could see no reason for Duclos' concern, but he didn't get paid to analyze. He was a typical bureaucrat who clocked in and out and was rather masterful at processing paperwork, but he had not a creative bone in his body or inspired thought in his head, although he would never admit to that.

"Roger that. Oh, and Étienne, there is something a bit odd I see going on with some of the migrants we're processing through this office."

"Odd how, Thierry?"

"Well, they seem to come up through Spain, originating from several of the north African countries, like Morocco and Tunis. They apply for residence permits as a family with all these kids."

"Migrants typically have big families, Jean. What's so unusual about that?"

"It's the families. They don't look like real families. The kids don't match as siblings. Different gene pools. And the way they relate to each other. Something's just off."

"That isn't much to go on, Thierry. Don't match! Since when are families supposed to look like a collection of Babushka nesting dolls? Seriously! Just get on to the Legionnaires." Click.

Thierry sighed. He knew he was onto something with the migrants but could not put his finger on it. And Brélot had been no help, as usual. Well, he had better get on to this latest assignment. At least it was something he would enjoy.

Thierry Jean set out for Allées Paul Riquet, a five-minute walk away. His destination was the restaurant/bar La Paillote, a somewhat shady looking establishment that attracted bikers and a seedier clientele. La Paillote means 'the hut', and the décor attempted a South-Sea-island ambiance in a tattered sort of way.

Looks can be deceiving, since La Paillote served up some of the best grilled mussels in the Languedoc and catered to night revelers with late-night food. La Paillote was also the venue for Gaspé, a bartender adroit at drinks and wit with his eveready répartées.

Signs of the Feria vendors setting up for the festival were everywhere on the promenade. Even though the event was a cash cow for the locals, Thierry dreaded the invasion to his normally laid- back town. In addition to tourists with money to burn, the festivities attracted gypsies who thrived on picking pockets and fleecing unsuspecting festival goers.

Migrants also seemed to show up in increased numbers, attracted by the music and over-all excitement. Thierry had a heartfelt concern for the migrants. They were vulnerable to being taken advantage of by unscrupulous persons Thierry did not want to see in his community. The human predators preying on the susceptible nomads were a dark form of evil that could only bring misery to mankind, and he sure did not want them in Béziers.

La Paillote was in quiet mode so early in the day, with most patrons sipping espressos or petit rouges, little glasses of red wine. From behind the bar Gaspé gave Thierry a nod of recognition and readied Thierry's customary noisette, an espresso with a dash of hot milk.

Gaspé was also the owner of La Paillote. In his 50's, he exuded the atmosphere that overflowed into his bar. There was a darkness about Gaspé that followed him like a perpetual dusk even at high noon. His eyes did not reflect light; rather, they seemed to absorb it, which cast shadows under his eyes that gave him the appearance of chronic sleep deprivation or a worn-out junkie.

From within the darkness of the bar came three sharp raps on a tabletop, followed by two longer ones. Al-gér-ie Fran-çaise. The calling card of the OAS. Thierry picked up his coffee and waded through the darkness until he spotted his contact, Old André, formerly of the OAS. You were never ex-OAS. You were either OAS or dead.

Somewhat toothless but perpetually grinning, one ear shot off and a left arm that refused to bend much, André had kept the faith of a French Algeria even though that train had long left the station. Almost eighty years old, André had become a fixture at La Paillote; it was far more welcoming and accommodating than his poorly heated bed-sit with grease-splattered wallpaper and plumbing that clanged when it worked, which was not consistently.

Gaspé had laid a clean mattress and blanket in a heated cubbyhole next to his bar's storeroom. With a toilet and slop sink adjacent to the cubby, a small refrigerator, and an armchair with sprung springs, André wordlessly but thankfully became La Paillote's guard dog after it closed in the wee hours.

His gnarled fingers wrapped around a petit rouge, his early-morning libation, André nodded for Thierry to join him.

"What brings you here so early in the day, Thierry Jean?"

Thierry signaled Gaspé for another small red wine for André and a basket of croissants.

"I heard the remains of two soldiers were found up near Cessenon-sur-Orb several days back. A Legionnaire found them. Know anything about that?" Thierry asked.

Gaspé arrived with the extras and paused to join in the conversation.

"Two Legionnaires, my friend," Gaspé corrected. "Believe me when I say you do not want to mess with them."

"They've been in here, Gaspé?"

The bar owner nodded.

"You hear anything?"

Gaspé shook his head. "Non, Thierry Jean. Whatever they are doing here they keep to themselves. But they are good customers. They bought the bar a round of drinks the other night. They had a young American with them."

"Do you know where they're staying in town?"

André spoke up. "The Mercure over on Saint-Saëns."

"You know this how?" Thierry asked.

André bristled at the doubt he heard in Thierry's voice. "Let's just say they aroused my curiosity, so I followed them."

"What else do you know about them, André?" Thierry pressed.

André fingered his petit rouge glass. He picked up the plastic stirrer Thierry had been given with his coffee.

"The big one could break you in half," he snapped the swizzle stick in two, "like that."

"Like I was saying," Gaspé said over his shoulder as he returned to the bar.

 "And someone else was tailing them, too."

"Any idea who?" Thierry asked.

"A Pied-Noir sympathizer named Karim", he answered matter-of-factly. "Actually, I think he's Harki."

"How do you know he is a Pied-Noir sympathizer?"

Old André took a long sip of his red wine and smacked his lips. "The Legionnaires caught him, didn't they?" He shuddered as he remembered what happened next. "Gilles Fouques' name was the last thing he screamed before the big one snapped his arm and put him unconscious. Left him in a heap down the side street near the Mercure. He's a mean bastard, that big Legionnaire."

*****

Thierry Jean lost no time in recruiting several of old André's younger associates to look into the movements of the two Legionnaires. His favorite uncle had been OAS and Thierry had a protective soft spot for the defunct faction. Both men Thierry chose were in their early forties, both sons of OAS paramilitary officers, and both still loyal to a dissident group the French government had mistakenly declared extinct decades ago.

Like a leviathan totally submerged except for bulging eyes, the OAS had gone underground in its activities, but it remained always watchful of the French leadership and which path it was taking the country down on any given day.

The Old Guard of the OAS had long since been decommissioned due to old age or death, André being a typical case in point. In fact, there were few left of those who had served in Algeria. But those to whom the baton had been passed, the young OAS, even though not trained soldiers like the older generation, were adamant in their protection of the French Republic.

*****

Chapter Ten

Claude Duclos placed a second call outside the DGSI chain of command to his contact on the Military Staff of the President of the Republic. Alexandre Chaumont was an enigma, a man in the shadows of the Élysée; he was also Duclos' back door to the president of France.

Fluent in Arabic, Chaumont was the son of Hervé Chaumont, a staunch Gaullist who had been the primary architect of De Gaulle's Algerian policy. Duclos' father, René, had served under Hervé Chaumont ... had, in fact, been Hervé's sounding board for some of France's off-book military interventions in Algeria, notably the massacre on Rue d'Isly.

The two men knew at the time the Algerian massacre went down that if word ever leaked out about their intentional and disastrous decision to use back woods Muslim troops resulting in French citizens being slaughtered like cattle it would, literally, bring down the French government, ruin De Gaulle and his legacy, and disgrace their family names forever. And worse.

General Ailleret had been silenced, as had Poupat, responsible for deploying the Muslim riflemen that day in Algiers. Their deaths, at the hands of René and Hervé, had been minor collateral damage to preserve the honor of two men whose family heritages carried the impeccable credentials of Saint-Cyr and Science Po in their backgrounds.

Claude Duclos and Alexandre Chaumont had grown up in the same social strata in Paris, attended the same schools, and become best friends, then lovers. Alexandre cut a dashing figure in Claude's life, and Claude felt honored that Alexandre had chosen him, even in intimacy.

The blissful union ended, however, when Claude's father ordered Claude to get married and begin raising a family.

"You've sown your wild oats," he thundered at his son. "It's about continuity. I want grandchildren. Marry Eveline Chaudoir and be done with it." Ever the obedient and intimidated son, Claude did what he was told.

Unwilling to accept a traditional career path like his lifelong friend, Alexandre spun off into the cloak-and-dagger world of clandestine arts. Alexandre Chaumont had ceased to exist to those who had known him, and Pierre Masoud emerged: handsome, suave, discreet, and very deadly.

He disappeared into the miasma of the Mideast where he thrived in the shadowy world of deception and crime, perfecting his Arabic and the needed skills to exist unnoticed while mastering the art of assassination. He operated on the fringe of the DGSE, almost a rogue agent, financed out of the French Prime Minister's special funds for Black Ops.

Masoud had been recalled to the Action Division of the DGSE located in the eastern suburb of Paris, Noisy-le-Sec, in 2017 where he became, once again, Alexandre Chaumont, advisor to the top tier of French government officials. Chaumont's metier, as he liked to think of it, was that of a fixer. A high-level fixer. And fix things he did, no matter the cost or method.

"Chaumont here."

Alexandre's voice momentarily gripped Claude Declos in an electric pathway from his heart to his genitals, but this sensation was immediately deadened by the situation at hand.

"It's Claude, Alex."

There was a moment's pause, then, "Ah, Claude. It's been a while. What can I do for you?"

That was Alex ... down to business.

"I just got a call from General Durand, National Gendarmerie. It seems the remains of two soldiers, one American, one French, have been found in the Hérault, north of Béziers." He waited for a response from Alex but when none came, continued. "Assassinated during the Algerian war."

This last provoked a response from Alex, a sharp intake of breath. "What are you saying?" he asked.

"It's the Rue d'Isly, Alex," he replied, "I'm sure of it."

"What! How?"

"Receding floodwaters exposed the remains." He paused. "There are two Foreign Legionnaires looking into it."

"Why the hell are Legionnaires poking into it?"

"That I don't know, Alex, but you realize where this could end up, right?"

The two men had always known their fathers' ill-chosen actions in Algiers could come back to bite them in the ass, but so much time had passed that the Rue d'Isly incident had long receded into the dark corner of the attic where discarded memories are carelessly stored. Now, like a sunken corpse suddenly released from the depths of water where it had been secured, popping to the surface, the distant slaughter of hundreds of countrymen had bobbed to the surface of the present where it could indict the past and condemn the future.

A low growl escaped Alex' throat. He knew only too well that being tied to these murders would, even one generation removed, ruin their respective families. The general public might not notice, caught up in their daily procession of trivia and basic survival, but the ancient lineages that carried France forward would crucify the family names of Duclos and Chaumont. They would forever be written out of the Who's Who of influential French families, cast as pariahs and untouchables.

*****

Chapter Eleven

Monday was an easy day for the bike group. They decided to visit the archaeological site of Oppidum d'Ensérune, the ancient Gallic village just outside Béziers.

"This settlement was a crossroads for several important land and sea routes," Hardy explained. "The Via Domitia, the old road that connected Rome to Cadiz, Spain, ran through here. It was a good location, strategically, as well. Elevated. Fertile land to farm. 360-degree view, and a water source."

"How long ago did people settle here?" Lilith asked.

"Records indicate the area was settled continuously from the 6th century BC to the 1st century AD."

"What are all these pits in the ground?" Fred asked.

"That's where they stored their food. The holes had covers, of course, and the rats and other vermin couldn't get at it." Hardy pointed to a large, deep, rectangular pit. "That was used for water storage. It's still capable of holding water to this day."

The group split up and spent an hour or so just exploring the site and the museum, which housed examples of pottery, tools, and weapons of the day. On their way out, Hardy stopped at a point overlooking a field below. The area was a large circle that looked like a bicycle wheel or pie, cut into wedges with a hole at the center.

"This used to be a swampy area. Monks drained the swamp in the 13th century by making these wedge-shaped fields separated by drainage ditches that drained the water toward the center. The water drained out a hole in the center and was carried off by an underground drainage system. That same system is still in use today."

"That must be where the term 'French drain' comes from," Harold said.

"Whatever," Delia muttered. She was done with old museum stuff.

The ride back to the Écluses des Fonseranes was an easy one and the crew arrived hungry and ready to eat. They assembled the food from their paniers, courtesy of Hotel XIX.

"Is this the French version of a Ploughman's lunch?" Geraldine asked.

The shredded and crispy duck, sliced ham, goat cheese, cornichons, onion chutney, rocket with balsamic vinaigrette, sprigs of red currants, and fresh baguettes spread out on the picnic table looked like a small feast.

"Typical French," Clive answered. "You have to admire the flavors and colors the hotel chef put together in our lunch. Far more sophisticated than the British counterpart. I've never known a field worker who ate duck with chutney."

*****

"According to my source in Langley, Kase Devine had been seconded to the CIA, which then sent him into Algeria for a boots-on-the-ground recon op. At the time, President Kennedy was supportive of Algeria's bid for independence. Langley thought it prudent to get a first-hand account of how the game was being played out in Algeria so he wouldn't end up with mud on his face or in a political pissing match with de Gaulle. Devine sent word that he was leaving Algeria with a defecting OAS operative, heading to a point of rendezvous here in the Hérault. They were assassinated before they reached their destination, presumably because they had information that could jeopardize de Gaulle's government and Algeria's push for independence."

Hardy had stopped by the Hotel Mercure after returning from the outing with his bike group and was listening intently to Alain's report and assessment.

"De Gaulle is long since gone, Alain, and Algeria's independence a done deal, so why is any of this still relevant today?"

Alain sighed. The intricacies of French politics could be difficult even for the French to follow.

"Yes, de Gaulle is gone, as you say, but his party is still very much alive and the largest political party in France. Sarkozy renamed the Gaullists in 2015 to the Republicans and the party has shifted more to the right, but is still a dominant force, politically. If it came out that le Grand Charles had an American operative and a French soldier killed to suppress information about the infamous slaughter on the Rue d'Isly or, worse, had orchestrated the slaughter, even now such a revelation could wrest the political majority from the Republicans and allow the radical left to form a coalition to rule."

"Could it have been someone other than de Gaulle who wanted the soldiers stopped?" Buvain asked.

Clotiers nodded. "It wouldn't have helped the FLN's image on the world stage if it were known they were responsible for cutting down elderly French citizens and children in cold blood during an otherwise peaceful demonstration. I've no doubt many world leaders, President Kennedy among them, would have denounced such brutality. The stakes were too high to let that happen." As an afterthought he added, "And the OAS couldn't just let one of their own defect and live to tell about it."

"So," said Hardy, "we have basically three factions who could've been responsible for the killings. Which one, do you think, is interested enough to put a tail on us?"

"Actually, we have a lead on that," Alain said. "Buvain caught someone following us last night and managed to extract some information from him under questioning."

Hardy winced involuntarily. He had seen Buvain question other victims, and the poor bastards usually ended up with something broken, somewhere. Buvain had a very heavy hand when it came to interrogation technique, with lots of screams to follow. Thus, the meaning of 'managed to extract …' He waited for Alain to continue.

"A young man named Karim, descendant of a Harki who made it out of Algeria during the war."

'Back to that damned war, again,' Hardy thought.

"What, exactly, is a Harki, Alain?" he asked. "You've used that expression before, and I don't know what it means."

"Harkis were Algerian Muslims who served as auxiliaries in the French Army during Algeria's War of Independence," Alain explained. "The term came to describe any Algerian Muslim who was in favor of a French Algeria. Their knowledge of the terrain in Algeria and the local customs were essential to the French trying to rule the country. Many of them were involved in intelligence gathering.

"When the peace accord with Algeria was signed the new masters agreed not to retaliate against the Harkis, but that was an empty promise. The paybacks began immediately, with Harkis and their entire families being gruesomely murdered, as many as 150,000 killed.

"De Gaulle ordered the French troops to prevent the Harkis from leaving for France, but many of the French officers disobeyed and helped the Harkis under their command, along with their families, to evacuate to the mainland. About 90,000 of them made it to safety, but the poor souls left behind were hunted down by their countrymen who killed them in diabolical ways. It was a horrific disaster and is a permanent stain on France's moral fabric. No amount of declarations or goodwill from various French leaders can ever erase it; a lot of people lost a lot. And the Harkis in France remain a largely un-assimilated refugee minority."

"So why would a Harki's son be following us around Béziers?" Hardy asked. "I don't get it."

"This Karim is tied in with the Jeune Pied-Noir in the area. They keep tabs on matters of interest to their community and finding these bodies is a matter of interest, but I don't think they pose a threat. They are merely curious … and still looking for a path to established recognition as sons of the Republic.

*****

"You took a terrible chance, my friend," Gilles Fouques admonished Karim Aboud as the two men sat in the shade of a large plane tree in the courtyard of Gilles' farmhouse. "Did you learn anything from it?"

Partially sedated, his left forearm in a fresh cast, Karim shook his head. "It all happened so fast," he said. The big Legionnaire was hiding on Rue Corneille and jumped me when I passed by. He pulled me into an alley to question me and this happened," he said, motioning with his broken appendage.

"Did you tell them anything, Karim?"

The Harki hung his head miserably. "My name," he said. "And that I was a Harki." "And that I worked for you."

*****

Chapter Twelve

The amphitheater in the Plateau des Poètes was soon filled by a steady trickle of people who had come for the first night of the flamenco performance. The murmurs of the crowd grew louder with excitement and anticipation as the hour approached for the entertainment to begin.

The stage was bare except for two large potted plants and a row of three chairs lined up at the back, with microphones set at each chair, and an amplifier. Facing the stage, the entrance for the performers at the back, right, was concealed by a large potted palm. A portable trailer, which served as a dressing room for the performers, was situated a short distance from the steps leading down from the back of the stage.

Without fanfare, a middle-aged man and woman, both somewhat overweight, took their seats in two of the chairs provided, followed by a younger man carrying his cypress-wood flamenco guitar. A hush fell on the audience as everyone held their breath, waiting.

The guitarist ran his fingers over the strings, producing a silky melody. Suddenly, Fania appeared dressed in a deep red dress with an hourglass fit at the top, her shapely shoulders and neck exposed, cut low in the back, with long, fitted sleeves ending in large black ruffles. From her slender waist the floor-length skirt swelled in fullness, with three rows of black ruffles spaced from her waist to the hem.

Poised and regal with her arms extended classically above her head and her hands clapping a soft rhythm, hips swaying, Fania let loose a few staccatos with her shoes, the toes and heels embedded with small nails to enhance her percussive footwork. Then, gathering herself to renewed height, her fine head in tune with a rhythm only she heard, she burst into a fury of pirouettes, twists, and turns, each one so controlled, so elegant it was impossible not to be enthralled, immediately.

The intensity with which Fania danced was like nothing Hardy had ever seen. Her dark eyes flashed and sank with raw emotion. Each movement was perfectly precise and graceful, her fluidity mesmerizing.

Fania's sensuality called to mind the sleek dance of classical Indian form, spiritual in its origins, a nod to the roots of Roma. Stylized yet highly personal, involving interpretive movements of fingers, hands, arms, upper torso, and intricate footwork. She appeared to have fallen into a transcendent emotional state, deeply focused, moving as a form of prayer. She danced profoundly, communicating with the audience and God.

The cantaor began his cante or song, equally a part of the flamenco performance. He sang with an anguish bordering on total despair, often no more than a plaintive wail. Sometimes the guitar player, or tocaore, accompanied the song, which took on a life of its own, with the dancer seeming to take a second place on the stage for the purpose of interpreting his song through her dance.

After what, to Hardy, seemed like forever the cantaor wound down, his voice now choking with emotion. The singer slumped back in his chair, physically drained. The audience broke out with cries of 'Olé' to honor his performance.

In an absolute torrent of lightening-speed staccatos, Fania swished the skirt of her dress from side to side with her hands in a crescendo, before pirouetting, arms held high with hands in scripted position, creating a drama of theatrical movement that held the audience in complete enchantment. Her maneuvers could have almost seemed violent in their passion but for the grace, refinement, and queenly decorum dictating her every action. It was a breathtaking performance and the audience rose to its feet amid calls of 'Olé' and thunderous applause in appreciation of the exquisite artist dancing before them.

She strode magnificently to the back of the stage and disappeared into her makeshift dressing room. In her absence the guitarist played a complicated piece accompanied by the spirited and steady clapping of the two singers.

The cantaora rose to her feet, still clapping rhythmically with the guitar, and launched into what undoubtedly was a tale of love forlorn, love done wrong, love unrequited. Her voice was somewhat husky and full of fervor as she pled her case of sorrow and grief.

Hardy did not particularly care for this aspect of flamenco. The singing just never moved him; he thought it forced and contrived, its plaintiveness almost a hoarse whine. Stylistically, he understood it, but he found he almost gritted his teeth as the performance went on, waiting for the dancing to recommence.

Finally, Fania remounted the steps to the stage, this time dressed in the traditional flamenco polka dots, black on pink with long sleeves and more ruffles and a magnificent, deeply fringed silk shawl covering her back and draped over her arms. Her dark hair was pulled tightly back into a braided knot at the nape of her neck with one tendril left as a perfect curl on her forehead.

At center stage she paused while the guitarist strummed silvery tones and the two cantaoras clapped lightly in sync. Her dark eyes, so intense, swept over her audience, consigning it to her mesmerizing power to enthrall.

In a slow movement that seemed to go on and on Fania swept the intricately embroidered shawl from her shoulders while turning her lithe body, creating an arc with her right arm as the scarf billowed majestically in its wake. Then, pulling the silk through her other hand as though threading a needle she took hold of its tail and began to swirl the luxurious fabric in an ever rapidly increasing circle until stopping, suddenly, to make her commanding eye contact with the audience. Then began a series of sharp staccatos with her feet, the shawl now draped over her shoulders and arms as she raised her ruffled skirt to showcase the amazing precision of her feet.

It was a thrilling performance, the audience completely under Fania's spell. The shawl became a cape which Fania, now a torero, or bullfighter, used to seduce, then antagonize an imaginary bull. Her arms were raised high over her head, the first and pinky fingers extended to become the bull's horns, and she charged by thrusting her hands dramatically down to each side, tossing her magnificent head, and thundering over the stage with her cleated shoes.

Following a final burst of shoe percussion with her arms stretched before her, covered by the shawl, Fania bowed elegantly and was on the verge of throwing a kiss to the crowd when a woman in the fourth row of VIP seating screamed. The man sitting next to her had been shot, and was slumped against her, dead.

An uproar ensued, with the audience dispersing in all directions. The police were summoned; they tried to prevent the stampede, but it was like trying to catch birds on the fly. Hardy, of course, remained calm. Casually, he made his way to the body, now sprawled in the chair, its head lolled back, unseeing eyes open. The dead man was Manuel Pirón.

*****

Back at the hotel the cycle group vacillated between nervous excitement and subdued shock while discussing the murder to which they had vicariously been a party. They recounted anything which could play a part in understanding what had happened.

"Wasn't the dead man the guy Fania introduced to us as her manager?" Lane asked.

"I thought he looked like a thug," Lilith commented. "He had an air of sleaze about him."

"I wonder what he was involved in, for someone to want him dead," Harold mused, half to himself.

Just then, Hardy entered the hotel's lobby, back from being questioned by the police, and the group rushed to greet him.

"What happened?"

"Did the police catch who killed him?"

"What did they ask?"

"What did you tell them?"

"Why did the police want to talk to you?"

A tired Hardy raised his hands defensively. "Mea culpa," he said in response to the last question.

"My first mistake was being found near the body when everyone else had beat it out of the amphitheater. My second mistake was volunteering that I knew the dead guy. When the police found out that I knew who he was they thought they had a live one. Unfortunately for them, that was as far as they could get, because I didn't know anything else."

"Who killed him?" Harold asked.

"No idea."

"How could he get shot with so many people around him?" Geraldine asked, almost indignantly.

"That's an easy one to answer," Hardy said. "He was shot during Fania's last heavy tap dance segment. No one heard the shot for the dancing. The police think the shooter must have been up in a tree behind the amphitheater because of the angle of the shot.

There were only four people on the stage, in plain view, and none of them fired the shot."

"Where is Fania?" Clive asked.

As if on cue, the dancer appeared, looking like she had been drugged, her queenly carriage gone. Her normally meticulous hair was straggly, with untamed wisps giving her a wild, unkept look. Her makeup was uneven, due to tears that had washed it away in some areas, with black smudges from her mascara adding to the overall damaged bearing.

The cycle group was stunned to silence by her appearance. In their eyes Fania had always seemed a svelte, charming goddess. This disheveled, broken-down woman was not even a caricature of her former self.

Fania felt the group's shock and revulsion at her presence, and she turned to leave, ashamed that anyone, especially strangers, should see her in her present state.

Hardy stepped forward. "Wait, Fania," he said, his voice commanding and gentle at the same time.

She hesitated, then turned back. Suddenly, she rushed at Hardy, throwing herself against him, sobbing like a child.

"I don't know anything," she sobbed. "The police think I'm somehow involved, but I don't know anything about Manuel's death."

No one said anything. Delia wasn't the only one who did a wide-eyed look.

*****

## Chapter Thirteen

News of Manuel Pirón's murder sent Gilles Fouques into a panic. First the two dead soldiers' remains being discovered, and now this. He felt like his universe was starting to career slightly off its axis, blurring the edges of his life. What could it all mean?

His friend, the mayor, had stopped by first thing on Tuesday morning with the announcement.

"You know anything about this Pirón's death, Gilles?" Henri Lecais wanted to know. Secretly, he feared Gilles had been part of it and he needed reassuring to the contrary.

"Non, Henri," he said, then realized what Henri was implying. He took umbrage at the thought.
"Non! Why would I do something like that, huh? And risk calling attention to myself?" He shook his head. "The list of people who wanted Pirón dead is undoubtedly a long one, but I'm not on it."

He looked out over his vine-covered hills, tinged red in color with the grapes to be harvested. It would take a crew of workers to pick the fruit at the optimal time. Without the labor of the migrant workers, he could lose his crop and a small fortune. His neighbors were in the same boat, relying on the transient pickers for a successful harvest.

Gilles would need to speak to his foreman, Karim, about the migrants. If they learned of Pirón's death some of them, especially the single men, might try to make a run for it which would leave the vintners in a bind during harvest.

A pickup followed by a cloud of dust announced Karim's arrival. The truck skidded to a stop and Karim sprang out, his face shrouded in a scowl.

"Nadim and his woman, Hafida, are gone," he said, "along with their two kids."

"What do you mean, gone?" Gilles asked.

"According to old Duma, they took off late last night with all their stuff. They had a ride waiting for them. Said something about heading for Toulouse."

A jolt of bile bit into Gilles at this bit of news. "Why would Nadim leave, Karim? Why now, so close to harvest?"

Karim levelled his gaze at Gilles, choosing his words carefully. "Perhaps it is because Señor Pirón threatened to put Hafida to work in Montpellier. She is a beautiful woman. Pirón thought her talents could be used better there."

"The fool!" Gilles spat. "Nadim must have been furious about it!" Fear took hold of Gilles. It began as a tiny ping caused by the realization that Manuel Pirón had been doing more than merely supplying workers for the grape harvest and spread over him in increasingly larger ripples as the reality of human trafficking took hold in his mind. How could he not have seen it?

The possibility that he was, somehow, involved with a human trafficker was anathema to him. Beyond his disgust at the thought, he was terrified that he would be accused of complicity in the crime of trafficking even though he was totally innocent.

Karim stood, scuffing the toe of his boot in the dirt, watching the small eddies of dust rise as he did so. When he looked up at Gilles he said, quietly and deliberately, "Nadim said he'd kill Pirón before he let him take Hafida."

"Karim, what else was Pirón doing with the migrants he brought to the Hérault?" He dreaded the answer, but he had to know.

"The men and most women were for the harvest," he replied. "He kept the families together, except the older kids were trained for the street. Pickpockets, begging.... And the young, attractive women went to work on the street."

*****

The gendarmes, as well as half a dozen Police Municipale, showed up at Hotel XIX early Tuesday morning demanding the key to Manuel Pirón's room. The local cops stood around outside the entrance trying to look useful but most of them were distracted, texting on their cell phones.

It was not a large room and the three gendarmes, who worked together as a team, divided up the space and went to work. Ten minutes later two of the investigators came up empty handed, but Lieutenant Lavigne, who had searched the contents of Pirón's desk, held up an old, stained, and tattered piece of paper like a trophy.

"This was inserted in his planner for today. Looks like it was written by Pirón's father, who claims to have been involved in the assassination of the two dead soldiers who turned up last week."

"Seriously?" his captain, Broussard, asked.

Lavigne nodded. "And something else, Capitaine. He tells his son his contact is an André Dubois, here in Béziers."

"That must be Old André who hangs out at La Paillote," Broussard said. "What's the connection between a cold case, a beat-up old warrior, and this Pirón guy?"

*****

Breakfast at the hotel the morning after Pirón's murder was suitably somber. The police had come and gone, making no effort to conceal their presence or mission. Hardy's group had trickled onto the terrace, the first stop being the coffee bar, then congregated around a large table the hotel had set to accommodate the cycling group. No matter where a conversation began, they all ended up discussing the previous evening's murder.

"I'm still just stunned that a murder was committed before our very eyes," Lilith said. Her fellow travelers echoed her sentiment.

"I've never seen a dead person before," Delia said, almost as a confession. She shuddered. "It's just so permanent," she added.

"Funny thing about being dead," Clive threw out crassly. He did not care that his comment made Delia wince. He was exasperated by the abysmal dimness of the woman.

Just then Lane appeared, entering the terrace from the street. "The cops have cordoned off the whole area around the stage in the park with crime-scene tape," he reported. "Even the trees along the path behind the stage are off limits, and there were a couple of police searching the ground under the trees and in the gardens lining the walkway. What's that about, Hardy?"

All eyes turned to Hardy. Where everyone else in the group had picked at their breakfast half-heartedly, Hardy was enjoying an impressive protein-heavy meal accompanied by the requisite croissants and fruits. When he turned towards Lane to respond the hotel cat, ever on the prowl, snagged a slice of ham off Hardy's plate and ran off with the catch swinging from his jowls.

"The shot that killed Pirón angled down from above where he was sitting. That leaves the stage, which they have ruled out for obvious reasons, and the area behind the stage, where they are searching. They'll look for footprints, signs of broken plants and branches, an area where tree bark has been scuffed ... they will especially look for the cartridge of the bullet that killed Pirón."

"Do the cops know what kind of gun was used?" Fred asked.

"They're not saying," Hardy replied, "but if I had to guess I'd say a low-caliber rifle, like a 22."

Fred nodded his agreement. "That sounds right," he said.

"How so?" Lilith wanted to know.

"Because," Fred explained, "if it had been a high-powered rifle it would have blown a hole the size of a dinner plate in Pirón's back where the bullet exited."

This graphic explanation put a definite damper on what remained of breakfast. Half an hour later, supplied with water and some fruit, the cycle group left for Narbonne, a charming town in the neighboring department of Aude, a two-hour ride south of Béziers.

Their destination was the picturesque area of Narbonne's centre ville, the old section of town where Narbonne's cathedral, an impressive Gothic building begun in 1272 but never finished, reigns over the walking-only area of Narbonne. The favorite site in Narbonne for everyone on the bike tour was an excavated portion of the ancient Via Domitia on the plaza near the Hôtel de Ville, or town hall.

For lunch Hardy had made reservations at the Grand Buffet, a phenomenon you could only experience in France. Clive was put off by the idea of a buffet and suggested another venue.

"Let's do this, Clive," Hardy said. "If, after you check out what the buffet has to offer you want to eat somewhere else, I'm good with that."

That seemed to mollify Clive. They arrived at the buffet early and were first in line, which meant they were in sight of the desserts, which featured a running fountain of melted chocolate surrounded by hundreds of confections, gateaux, tartes, tortes, mousses ... anything and everything you could dream of to finish off a meal. The amount of fresh whipped cream on display was lethal. Still, Clive was not convinced.

With permission from a chef wearing a full toque, Hardy steered Clive over to the fresh seafood display.    Artfully arranged pyramids of fresh shrimp, crabs, crab legs, and combinations and concoctions only a French chef could create covered an enormous portion of the buffet.

"If you prefer, Clive, the chefs will prepare a lobster to your specifications," Hardy told him.    He guided Clive over to the special-order area where chefs waited to prepare anything you did not see in the buffet.    They walked past classic French entrées of blanquette de veau, beef burgundy, rôti de porc, coq au vin, frog legs, shrimp, escargot, salmon, and assorted vegetable dishes.    The charcuterie display boasted six different legs of ham from various locales, assorted foie gras… it was truly staggering.

"And the cheese area has over one hundred selections, Clive," he said, pointing toward the fantastic collection of fromages.    "It is actually listed in the Guinness Book of World Records."

Clive was actually humbled by what he saw.    "I'm in," he said.

From Narbonne, the group cycled to Les Cabanes de Fleury, a remote and uncrowded beach on the Mediterranean where the Aude River, which began in the Pyrénées Mountains, emptied into the sea.    It was a relaxing ride on full stomachs through hilly scrubland and cultivated vines along narrow back roads that met up with the river and followed it to its mouth.    After soaking up some sun, the sated travelers lazily began the ride back to Béziers, expecting to arrive in time for a shower and change before a light dinner.

*****

Chapter Fourteen

Alexandre Chaumont, in the persona of Pierre Masoud, had arrived in Béziers in time for a late lunch at the tapas restaurant, Pica-Pica, then checked into a comfortable room facing the Jean Jaurès plaza at the adjoining XIX Hotel. The desk clerk at the hotel noted Masoud's monogrammed Berluti leather carry-on and the Nomos Lambda Roségold watch on his left wrist and decided he was probably the owner of the teal-colored Aston Martin that had disappeared into the underground parking garage a few minutes earlier.

Chaumont had shed his skin of officialdom and molted into the operative mode of Masoud. Handsome in an undefined manner. Sleek, but not oily. This man, Pierre Masoud, appeared a well-bred, mild-mannered man in his early forties. It always shocked his prey when the gentleman they beheld struck with the lightning speed of the assassin he was.

"I thought Béziers was a sleepy little town in the South of France," Masoud said, making conversation with the desk clerk. "Is there a celebration going on?"

The clerk took on an air of self-importance at being able to offer something to his wealthy guest. "The Feria is on this week," he replied. "Bull fights, flamenco, music, street parties … oh, uh, and there was a man murdered last night at the flamenco performance." He blushed when he realized he probably should not have announced this but was rewarded when the well-dressed stranger's ears pricked up.

"A murder, you say? What was that about?"

The clerk shrugged. "No one knows, but the murdered man was staying in this hotel. The police were here early this morning searching his room."

Masoud saw an opportunity. "Didn't I read that there were two bodies found near here just last week? Washed up by the recent flood?"

An edge to the stranger's voice raised a red flag of caution in the clerk and he merely nodded but said no more. He finished processing the check-in and handed the heavy brass key to his guest. "Room 306, Sir. The elevator is to your right; breakfast begins at 7:00."

Pierre had time to kill before the rendezvous Claude Duclos had set up with his Béziers contact, so he wandered over to explore the Allées Paul Riquet that was awash with humanity having a good time.

A small troupe of clowns on stilts tentatively kept their balance on the uneven tarmac as kids ran helter-skelter, some darting between their splinter-like legs. A smiling balloon man with a fist full of strings attached to a cloud of inflated shapes overhead kept to the center of the Allées, thus avoiding the branches of the plane trees that seemed to reach for his fragile merchandise.

Hundreds of people, seated at tables placed on the edge of the Allées, ate pizza, bratwurst in buns, kebabs, grilled meats, and paella, while consuming beer sold in various-sized glasses and wine dispatched from booths set up by the Occitanie area's most notable vineyards. Rock music throbbed from a band performing in front of the theatre at the top of the Allées.

Exactly at 16:00 hours he slipped through the entrance of La Paillote, overstepping the small fawn-colored dog that lay sleeping in the middle of the sidewalk, oblivious to all passersby. He paused, allowing his eyes to adjust to the darkened interior. The bar was empty except for Gaspé, who kept busy carrying drinks to the customers sitting at his tables across the narrow Allées on the promenade, an old man who had fallen asleep where he sat, his head resting on the table while he still clutched his glass of wine, and a middle-aged man waiting for Pierre, Thierry Jean.

"This town has a lot to offer for a first-time visitor," Pierre remarked, sitting opposite Thierry Jean.

"It definitely is not for the frivolous," Jean replied, correctly giving the expected code response. He felt a bit silly, playing spy, but at the same time there was a thrill to it all.

Pierre sat a moment, surveying the interior of the bar, studying Thierry, and noting the old man snoring softly at the nearby table. He gave a slight nod.

"Pierre Masoud?" Thierry asked.

His question went unanswered, but Masoud stiffened at mention of his name.

"Claude Duclos called me earlier; told me to meet you," Thierry persisted.

"What can you tell me about the Legionnaires?" Masoud asked. He was irritated by this stupid man who gave out names without thinking.

"You want something to drink?" Thierry asked.

The slight shake of Pierre's sleek head was serpentine; something about this person made Thierry Jean's skin crawl.

"The men you are looking for have rooms at the Hotel Mercure," Thierry said. "They've been asking a lot of questions. There is a young American with them, sometimes, and one of the dead men had an old film of a document that they viewed at the Médiatheque."

"Have you seen them?"

Thierry nodded. "They come here sometimes for a drink. I put two men on them to see where they go and who they talk to."

"Anything?" Pierre asked.

Thierry Jean shook his head.

"Where's this hotel where they are staying?"

"Down Saint-Saëns, off the other side of the promenade, midway," Thierry answered. "You need me to do something for you?"

Masoud shook his head, said nothing.

"What are you going to do?" Thierry wanted to know.

Masoud's head jerked slightly; his eyes bore into Thierry's. "It's best you don't know," he hissed.

The old man, still asleep, gave a loud snort, then his snoring resumed its steady rhythm.

Pierre nodded at the old man. "Who is he?"

Thierry gave what he hoped was a careless glance at Old André before answering.

"He's just an old wino who is a fixture in Béziers. Harmless. And a bit crazy."

Pierre said nothing. He gave a last, quick look at the slumbering old man, nodded at Thierry, and was gone.

Relief flooded Thierry; this man, Masoud, was a bad man, he could tell. He hoped he had seen the last of him, but a foreboding said otherwise. He gave Old André a protective look; perhaps the old man should disappear for a while.

Old André, who had only feigned sleep while listening to the two men talk, felt the same way. But there was something he must do first.

*****

## Chapter Fifteen

Using his hand to shield his eyes from the setting sun's glare Tuesday evening, Gilles Fouques watched a faded red Jeep Cherokee bounce its way up the lane to his farmhouse. When two men, one of them built like a brick shithouse, exited the vehicle Gilles knew, instantly, who his visitors were.

"Gilles Fouques?" Clotiers asked.

Gilles nodded. It would be pointless to do otherwise. The other man, large and bear-like, had moved around behind Gilles, an action that made Gilles more than a tad nervous in light of what had happened to Karim's ruined arm.

Sensing his tension Clotiers said, "My name is Alain Clotiers; this is Luc Buvain. We mean you no harm; we just want to talk to you."

"Lucky me," Gilles spat. "Is that what you told Karim last night, also?

He sensed Buvain move a step closer to his back … saw Clotiers give a short shake of his head.

"It was unfortunate what happened to Karim. When he refused to cooperate Buvain got a little heavy handed."

Clotiers paused to look around him. Fields of soon ready-to-be-picked sun-kissed grapes, their clusters heavy on rows of meticulously kept vines rising and falling on the hill sides as far as the eye could see. There was an ancient order defined by the vines that was comforting in its steadfastness.

The old mas, or farmhouse, that Gilles Fouques called home had been built in the shape of a U out of local stone with the honey-gold colored rock prolific in the South of France, resembling a Spanish hacienda. The rear of the building faced the direction of the prominent wind in the area, in this locale the Tramontane, and had no windows. Unless one has lived in the path of the Mistral or Tramontane one cannot appreciate this simple gesture of architecture as a defense against the relentless beatdown of the wind.

Traditionally, these farms were very self-sufficient, producing their own fruits, vegetables, meat, grain, milk, and even silkworms, in earlier times. The stables took up one side of the U and were a bit run-down, truth be told. Gilles was not a gentleman farmer with an equestrian streak, so the stables had been given over to a few chickens and storage of viticulture paraphernalia. The other side of the U was home to several pigs for fattening, a small flock of sheep, a handful of goats, and a milk cow.

The middle section housed Gilles and his family. It was a comfortable abode but still functioned as a farmer's home, unlike many of the Languedoc mas that had been bought by British expats and refurbished to an entirely different comfort level.

"Did your father, Gaspard, live here after he left Algeria?" Clotiers asked.

The question startled Gilles. "You knew my father?" he replied.

"He was an OAS sympathizer, I believe …"

"No!" Gilles shouted. "Not true! Just because he was a Pied-Noir did not mean he was in league with the OAS. No, my father hated violence from all quarters. He was mindful that the OAS and Pied-Noir had the same goal, a French Algeria, but he did not approve of the methods employed by the para group."

"This mas was a safe house for those who fled Algeria," Clotiers said, trying a new tack.

Gilles nodded. Suddenly, memories flooded through him of late-night guests arriving, of finding strangers, whole families, even, in the stable at morning's light with his mother busy in the great kitchen fixing food enough for a small army …

"Two soldiers heading to this destination many years ago were murdered near the bridge at Réals …. But I'm telling you something you already know, yes?"

Gilles nodded, then looked at Clotiers directly and nodded, again.

"So, what I am wondering, Gilles Fouques, is why you had Karim following us around Béziers?"

Anger reared up in Gilles. "Who are you, Alain Clotiers, to question me? You and this thug (he glanced over his shoulder at Buvain) who maims people for no reason. Why have you come to my home? What do you think I have to tell you?"

Silently, Buvain moved from behind Gilles and stood next to Clotiers, looking like his pet bear. Clotiers shrugged his shoulders, then relaxed. He removed his sunglasses and stepped into the shade of a large plane tree at the courtyard's entrance.

"I am Lieutenant-Colonel Alain Clotiers, 2nd Para Regiment out of Calvi, Corsica. And this is Captain Luc Buvain from the same." He briefly flashed his military ID for Fouques, then continued.

"A colleague of ours found the remains of two assassinated soldiers last week at the Orb River and …"

"Would this be the American bike tour operator," Gilles interrupted.

Clotiers hid his surprise when he answered. "Yes." Then, "You are remarkably well informed, M Fouques."

Fouques said nothing.

Clotiers continued. "We believe the two dead men, one French, the other, American, fled the war in Algeria with information that could shed light on an unfortunate incident that took place in Algeria. We believe they were killed to prevent this information being made public. We are trying to find out who killed them."

Gilles Fouques listened impassively to Clotiers and, when he had finished, asked, "Did the film you took from one of the bodies provide any information about that?"

The astonishment on Clotiers' face evoked a wry smile from Gilles, then his face sobered.

"Even now, those of us who are descendants of the many thousands who fled Algeria watch our backs, Colonel. You see many peaceful hectares of vines and an isolated farm in the secluded Languedoc hinterland, but underneath there is a raw wariness whose nose sniffs for scents of betrayal and danger. I am a Jeune Pied-Noir and will forever be. Karim is Harki, through and through."

"And the OAS?" Buvain snarled.

"They, too, have eyes," Gilles said.

"Does Old André have ties to OAS?" Clotiers pressed.

Gilles' face remained impassive except for a nervous flicker of his eyes. He said nothing.

"You still haven't answered my question, Gilles Fouques, as to why your buddy, Karim, was following us," Clotiers said.

For an instant Gilles squeezed his eyes shut, his face placid. When he opened them, he said, only, "Yes, I have, Colonel."

As Clotiers and Buvain made their way down the winding dusty lane from the Fouques farm they passed a bunkhouse structure they had not noticed earlier. They saw it now due in large part to several straggly-looking children who had been watching the road for their return but ducked shyly back inside the low building to avoid being seen as the Jeep Cherokee drove past.

"Looks like migrant kids," Buvain commented.

"They do, indeed, Buvain. Who do you think works the vendange? The real question is, are they here legally?"

Neither Legionnaire mentioned the motorbike that appeared out of nowhere and kept a steady distance from the Jeep as it headed back to Béziers.

*****

## Chapter Sixteen

Old André saw the Jeep Cherokee turn into the underground parking garage on Jean Jaurès and waited for the two Legionnaires on the landing to the first level of the garage, out of sight of anyone watching from the Allées and surroundings. It was risky, but something he had to do. He could hear the two men ascending the cement stairs from below.

Clotiers and Buvain stopped when they saw the old man, apparently waiting for them on the landing above them. He was a pitiful sight when seen outside La Paillote. Here, he appeared shrunken, almost fragile. He stood wringing his hands, glancing constantly up to the street-level entrance as though he were being hunted.

"Evening, André," Clotiers said by way of greeting.

"What's up, André?" Buvain asked, a bit gruffly.

The old man coughed to clear his throat. "A man, Pierre Masoud, is in town, asking about you," he said. His rheumy eyes were tinged with fear. "He is a bad man, Monsieur Clotiers. He means you harm."

Instinctively, Buvain moved closer to his boss.

"How do you know this, André?" Clotiers asked.

"He was in La Paillote this afternoon, meeting with the Sous-Prefect, Thierry Jean."

"Why would this man meet with the Sous-Prefect?" Clotiers asked.

"Thierry is part of a network of informants for the DGSI run by a man named Claude Duclos. Duclos sent this man, this Masoud, to meet with Thierry."

"What did Thierry Jean tell this man?" Buvain asked.

The old soldier swung his head to look at the giant Legionnaire. He shuddered at the memory of Karim's arm snapping. Buvain, he knew, could kill him with one swat, but as long as Clotiers had the warrior on a leash Old André felt safe.

"He told him where you were staying. That there was an American with you. And that you had a film from the dead men you found."

Clotiers was stunned by this information. He closed his eyes momentarily to hide the spasm of alarm jolting him. He wondered, wryly, how many others in Beziers knew. Then, smiling, he pulled a money clip from his pants pocket, peeled off ten fifty-euro notes, and handed them to the old soldier.

"Thanks, my friend," he told André. "Take this and lay low for a while. If you have a place to stay out of Béziers, go there. And do not tell anyone where you've gone, not even Gaspé. Go now."

The old man gratefully stuffed the money in his pocket and entered the first level of the parking garage. He would exit by the elevator on the other side of Jean Jaurès plaza, nowhere near Clotiers and Buvain, and disappear as suggested, but first he needed to make a quick stop by his wretched studio. That done, he made a detour to La Paillote to let Gaspé know he would be gone for a while without saying where to. It was the least he could do.

André took the first train out of the Béziers station heading east toward Montpellier. Five stops later, he boarded another train heading for Toulouse, reversing his direction. The wily old soldier observed no one following him and, when he arrived in Narbonne, he disembarked and left the   station.

The Legionnaires went directly to the Hotel Mercure in a heightened sense of awareness. They said nothing until they were in Clotiers' room. Buvain did a quick sweep for listening devices, found none, and gave Clotiers the nod.

Clotiers placed a call to an old friend, Damien Barjols, who was an analyst in the DGSI, Paris.

The call was picked up on the first ring. "Barjols."

"Damien… Alain Clotiers."

"Clotiers, you old boudin! How goes it?" Damien never missed an opportunity to take a dig at Clotiers with his 'boudin' comment … a joke at the bedrolls Legionnaires carried that looked like sausages.

Clotiers laughed, in spite of himself. Highly intelligent and a bit of a geek, Damien Barjols let few people see his sense of humor and Clotiers considered it a mark of their friendship that he was one of the few.

"How are Marjorie and the kids?" Alain asked. Clotiers appreciated Damien's wife and kids, though he had neither and did not feel as if he had missed much in staying single.

"Oh, you know … she keeps me in line, and Amélie and Christian are at university. They cost me a packet, but they are worth every sou." Damien paused. "But you didn't call me to talk about such things, Alain. What mission are you on now, and how can I help you?"

"Take a walk outside, Damien; I'll call you in five."

When Damien's personal cell phone rang a few minutes later he answered it with, "What shit pile have you stepped in now, Alain?"

"Claude Duclos and Pierre Masoud. What can you tell me about these men?"

Damien let out a low whistle. "I have to hand it to you, old friend. That's quite a pair of devils."

"How so?"

"Duclos and Masoud are lifelong friends. Both come from French elite society. The usual: Saint-Cyr, Science Po …. Both fathers were high-ranking, served under De Gaulle during the Algerian situation …"

"Tell me about that, Damien," Alain interrupted. "What about Algeria?"

Damien pursed his lips in thought as he searched his memory for the Algeria file stored in his brain. "Well," he began, "Chaumont was the senior officer advising de Gaulle about his Algerian offensive and Duclos was under him. The two ran some dicey black ops during the war that didn't end up very well for France."

"Such as?"

"That's just it, Alain. There were always whispers about their ops but nothing definite."

"Anything about the Rue d'Isly massacre?"

Damien held his breath. "Cripes, Alain!" he exploded. "When that fiasco went down there was initial finger pointing at Chaumont, but suddenly two generals involved in the disaster died … rather suspiciously, I might add … and that was the last of the finger pointing. Oh, and by the way, Pierre Masoud is really Alexandre Chaumont, General Chaumont's son."

"Why the Pierre Masoud, then?" Clotiers asked.

"A bit of a mystery. Lots of rumors. Chaumont's gay lover jilted him, so he transferred to Babylon and trained as an assassin. A ninja of some sort. Involved in some nasty stuff while in the Mideast. Been back in Paris less than a year and works out of the DGSE in a vague capacity. Runs his own game, it seems. He cleans up messes for the high-ups, among other things."

Alain was silent while he processed all the information Damien had dumped on him. It would take some sorting out, but of one thing he was certain: the situation in Béziers was about to get intense.

"Can you send a picture of this Chaumont/Masoud to my phone, Damien?"

"Will do, Alain."

He thanked his friend for his help and was just about to ring off when a thought came to his head. "Damien, who was the lover who dumped Chaumont?"

"Claude Duclos. Needs be careful with this one, Alain."

Buvain listened intently as Alain recounted his conversation with Damien Barjols. A chirp from his phone told Alain the promised picture of the assassin had been received. He and Buvain studied the refined-looking man in a tailored suit and tried to imagine him in combat.

"A bloody poofter!" Buvain joked.

"Non, Buvain," he admonished. "He may be gay, but he is indeed deadly."

"Well, we know what he looks like, but he has no idea who we are," Buvain said.

"For now, Buvain," Clotiers agreed.

*****

Back at the hotel in Béziers, after the daytrip to Narbonne, Hardy heard Fania's tinkling laughter erupt from the hotel's bar as he passed the entrance on the way to his room. Glancing in, he noted the sleek head coquettishly cocked as she gazed into the face of a handsome stranger who, Hardy thought, looked somewhat bored at the game she was playing with him. He stood at the bar, fingering his room key, indicating an impatience to escape. Around five-foot-ten and compact, even from this distance Hardy could see a man physically fit and coiled like a taut spring.

Fania cast a quick glance in Hardy's direction and turned up the charm on her audience, ostensibly in an effort to make Hardy jealous. 'Ridiculous woman,' Hardy thought, taking the stairs to his room. After a quick shower to remove the road dirt, sweat, and sand, Hardy headed over to the Hotel Mercure for an update with Clotiers and Buvain.

The response to Hardy's knock at Clotiers' door caused a bustle of activity: Clotiers stuffed a nine-millimeter automatic in the rear waistband of his pants and Buvain palmed a small throwing knife.

"Who is it?" Clotiers demanded.

"It's me, Hardy."

The door opened immediately, and Hardy noticed relief relax Clotiers' expression and, when Clotiers turned back into his room, he saw the pistol lodged at his waist. The questioning look he sent Buvain was met with Buvain moving from at-ease while re-sheathing his knife.

"What the hell is going on, Alain?" Hardy asked, alarmed.

"There have been some developments, mon ami," he replied. "It seems a person of interest, a dangerous person of interest, has come to town asking about Buvain and me."

"Who is this person of interest?"

Alain thrust his phone toward Hardy. "This man," he said. "An assassin whose father, it seems, had much to do with the Rue d'Isly disaster and, most probably, the murder of our two soldiers."

Hardy studied the image of the man on Alain's phone. Dark eyes, intense looking. He was slightly heavier now, his hair had a touch of silver, and he was sporting a neatly kept goatee, but it was the same man.

"I just saw this guy," he told them. "He appears to be staying at my hotel."

Alain gave Hardy a long look. "As tempting as it may be for you to check this guy out, Hardy, I am asking you to please stay away from him. He is, by all accounts, a highly trained and ruthless killer. Out of your league. Promise me you will not get involved with him."

Hardy managed a vague nod of agreement. "Yeah, sure."

"By the way, do you know anything about the murder last night at the Flamenco performance?" Alain asked.

Hardy shook his head. "I was there. The cops questioned me, but I really have no idea what it's about, Alain. The police searched the victim's room at my hotel this morning and discovered an old letter apparently written by the dead man's father mentioning someone named André Dubois."

"And you know this how, my friend?" Alain asked.

"My room is next to the murder victim's and the police assumed I didn't understand French."

Alain shot a glance at Buvain, who nodded. None of this was lost on Hardy.

"What's up, Alain?" he asked.

"This André Dubois is an old soldier who was part of the OAS back in the day. Probably still is. He is a fixture at La Paillote, a bar we know on the Allées. It was André who alerted us to this Chaumont/Masoud person asking around about the 'two Legionnaires.'"

"How did he come across that information?" Hardy wanted to know.

"Eavesdropping on a conversation in La Paillote. I gave him some cash for his intel and told him to leave town and lay low for a while. Assassins typically do not leave loose ends."

*****

Chapter Seventeen

Wednesday was the day the bike tour had planned to visit the fortified medieval citadel, the Cité of Carcassonne. The group boarded a chartered van in Béziers for the hour-long ride to the walled town, arriving just after 10 AM. There was a bustling crowd heading for the entrance gate and tourists already strolled the ramparts, enjoying the views out over the plain below.

The group gathered around Hardy in the parking lot outside the Narbonne Gate, one of the four ancient remaining gates giving access into the Cité. He gave everyone a map of the citadel and an introductory speech.

"This Oppidum is about the same age as the one we saw near Béziers, though much larger," Hardy explained. "It was strategically important because it straddles two trading routes: between the Mediterranean and Atlantic, and the Massif Central and the Pyrénées. Of note, the Cathars were expelled from here in 1209, and one of the towers in the fortress was used during the Inquisition. The French government decided to tear the fortress down in 1849, but cooler heads prevailed. Fortunately, and it was restored, instead.

"It is one of France's top tourist destinations so it will be crowded, and there is an abundance of souvenir shops and more than the usual claptrap. I suggest we split up to explore the town and meet for cassoulet at the restaurant Comte Roger on Rue Saint-Louis at one o'clock. I've marked it on your maps. It's just down the street from the Best Western. There is an open-air patio in the back of the restaurant where I've made reservations for the group."

Hardy's group set off as one to explore the fortified city but soon fragmented as everyone found something to claim his attention. The endless press of tourists trudging the narrow streets and filling the souvenir and trinket shops helped to disperse the cyclists. Shops selling candles, wind chimes, barrels of candy, soaps, fake knight armor and weapons, family crests, local food specialties, silly period costumes, modern boutiques, restaurants, smoothie bars, cafes, hotels, and an endless array of stuff in the category of everything you could want but nothing you need.

Lunch in the garden of Comte Roger was a sigh of relief for the footworn travelers. They were accustomed to less densely touristed places to explore and the allure of the Cité, though appreciated, had worn thin quickly. The tinkling of the fountain and subdued sounds of dining were an invitation of good things to come.

"So, what's the local specialty this restaurant serves?" Fred asked, rubbing his hands in anticipation.

"It's called cassoulet," Hardy responded. "It started out as a farmer's dish, a simple winter stew, but has been elevated to gourmet status."

"Kinda like beef burgundy?" Lane asked.

"Exactly," Clive chimed in. "As only the French can do."

"What does that mean?" Delia wanted to know. "What, exactly, is cassoulet?"

"Here in Carcassonne one of the key ingredients in the stew is red partridge in addition to pork, tomatoes, and carrots, along with the ubiquitous white beans, of course. Sometimes the partridge will be replaced by mutton. In Castelnaudary, just up the road, fresh pork or ham is used, with more garlic. And Toulouse, which loves to claim cassoulet as its own, uses duck and goose confit along with Toulouse sausage. The goose fat makes the dish almost too rich to eat."

It was decided. The entire group ordered the house cassoulet, paired with a hearty red wine from the Minervois. Hardy recommended a small salad on the side.

"Otherwise, you get overwhelmed with the stew, it's so rich."

The diners attacked their cassoulets with gusto, enjoying the subtle complexities of the stew. After several minutes, however, the fervor became a slog, then a challenge to finish the rich dish.

Delia summed up the group's sentiment when she threw down her fork and gasped, "It's delicious, but I just can't eat any more of this!"

*****

Late Wednesday morning Fania took a taxi to Gilles Fouque's farm. She found the vintner cleaning his sprayer after applying a final application of copper to keep powdery mildew at bay from his precious vines. Gilles glanced up as the taxi stopped in his dooryard. When he saw who alighted from the vehicle he swore under his breath. This woman was bad news.

Fania sauntered over to where Gilles worked, being careful that the copper-tinged water did not splash her shoes. Her eyes took in the stone house with its annexes, the surrounding vineyards, and a yellow dog slumbering in the shade of a plane tree overhanging the tool shed.

"I'm looking for a husband and wife we brought here last month," she said. "They had two small children, a boy and a girl."

"That's not much to go on. Lots of migrants pass through here. Describe them."

"I have no idea what they look like. Pirón handled them. Don't all migrants look the same?"

Gilles paused with his task, a concentrated look settling on his face. After several moments he shook his head and went back to his cleaning. "Not here," he said. "The only family I know of are gone. They left a few nights ago and haven't been back. Word has it they've gone to Toulouse. Not sure it's who you're looking for."

"What? No!" Fania fairly shouted. "It must be the same migrants. How could you let that happen? I have money invested in that family!"

Gilles finished what he was doing and turned off the hose, acting like she was not even there.

"Pirón is dead," Fania informed him coldly. "It is now my operation. You will deal directly with me."

"What happened to Manuel?" Gilles asked.

"I didn't know you were on a first name basis with him," she countered.

He ignored the jibe; repeated his question.

"Someone shot him during my flamenco performance Monday evening," Fania said, tossing her coiffed head.

"How convenient. That leaves you with a thriving but nasty business. Are you sure you are up to getting those graceful hands dirty?"

"You needn't concern yourself about my hands, Fouques. Just find my damned migrants. I'll be in touch." The taxi sped back the way it had come, carrying Fania, in a cloud of Languedoc dust.

Her last words seemed almost a threat. He thought, briefly, of Pirón. 'You poor bastard; that's what happens when you dance with the devil.'

A woman appeared from the annex building where she had been hiding and listening to the exchange between Gilles and the flamenco dancer.

"You heard?" Gilles asked, nodding in the direction of the disappearing taxi.

"Thank you for not giving us up to her."

"You heard what she said about Pirón?" He paused, then asked, "Did you have anything to do with his death, Hafida?"

The woman stiffened. "No, Gilles. He was only the tip of the spear; it is she who poisoned the tip and thrust it." Hafida nodded. "She is a wicked woman, Gilles. She can only bring you trouble."

Fouques pursed his lips, knowing Hafida spoke the truth. He was over a barrel. He needed a supply of migrants to work his vines and Pirón had met that need for years with a minimum of distress. With him dead, the landscape had changed, drastically. Pirón had been a businessman; Fania was greedy, and greed led to rash, foolish decisions.

The idea of dealing with someone who had no problem putting a married woman with children on the street as a prostitute revolted him. His moral compass heaved at the prospect of relying on such a person to supply him migrants to work his vineyards. In no way did he want to be complicit in any form of human trafficking.

*****

Chapter Eighteen

Hardy was late for his coffee date with Fania late Wednesday afternoon when he got back from the daytrip to Carcassonne. He did not really think of it as a date, but she, apparently, did, and she was none too pleased at his tardiness.

"Sorry I'm late," he said, sliding into his chair on the terrace of Le Cristal.

Fania sniffed at his apology, her lips in a small moue.

Hardy was put off by her pretense. As far as he was concerned, they were mere acquaintances thrown together by circumstance, not lovers having an assignation. He just didn't do the games-women-play well, at all; life was too short for such nonsense.

The waiter, François, stopped at their table, pen poised to take their order.

"What will you have, Fania?" Hardy asked.

"Campari Spritz," she said, with a dismissive wave of her hand. Her behavior embarrassed Hardy.

"I'll have a café grand, please," he said. He hesitated. "Are you still serving café gourmand?"

François gave a short nod with his head.

"Great! Change that to a café gourmand with a café grand."

When the waiter had gone with their order an embarrassed silence descended on their table, finally broken by Fania.

"I don't know what to do, Hardy," she said.

"About …?"

She waved her hands expressively to include an ambiguous quantity.

"This situation with Pirón."

"You mean his murder, Fania?" Hardy replied.

She seemed to recoil, caught herself.

"Yes, his murder. Exactly."

"What about it?" Hardy persisted.

She appeared to be sorting through her options to reply and chose one.

"Well, do I have to stay here, in Béziers? I really should return to Spain to prepare for my next appearance. Are the police done questioning me?"

"Did they tell you that you could leave? Normally, in an ongoing investigation in the early stage, at least, they want witnesses to stick around."

"But I didn't witness anything," she protested.

"Didn't you?" Hardy countered. "The victim was sitting right in front of you. You didn't notice anything?"

"How could I? I was ending my shawl dance and totally absorbed in my performance."

"Why was Pirón in Béziers, anyway? Did he normally accompany you to your performance destinations?

"Not normally, no," she replied. "His appearance in Béziers was totally unexpected. He said something about looking up an old friend of his father was the reason he came here."

"Did you and Pirón get along, Fania?" Hardy asked, changing gears.

She was somewhat taken aback by his directness.

"What do you mean?" She was stalling for time to form her response.

"Did you like him? Was he a good manager, or one of those who only wanted to suck you dry for his monetary gain?"

"Why are you asking me this, Hardy?" Fania said, slightly flushed. "What is this questioning? Do you think I had something to do with his death?" She was starting to get a little shrill.

Hardy shook his head. "No, of course not, Fania," he assured her. 'At least I didn't, until now,' he thought. There was something very unsettling about the panic he felt coming from the dancer. He could almost see it rising in her like the mercury in a thermometer.

As if on cue, their orders arrived and Fania dove into her drink while Hardy started sampling his various mini desserts. He offered Fania a taste of her choice, but she demurely refused, citing the need to rein in her waistline or buy a new flamenco wardrobe.

"They look like migrants," Fania announced, pointing toward a family of assorted ages and sizes with her swizzle stick. "We get a lot of them passing through Spain on their way to the rest of Europe. Some stay in Spain and work as day laborers, but they compete with the local unskilled workers and there is a lot of resentment toward them, so they move on. I imagine they get work around here during grape harvest."

Hardy looked to where she had pointed. A large group consisting of four adults and a swarm of children, brightly but shabbily dressed, their skin light with rose tones, hovered near the statue of Pierre-Paul Riquet that dominated the area, about fifty feet from their table. The setting sun shining in his eyes made it difficult to see much in detail.

The children, in a range of ages, chased one another through the fountain, splashing in the water, scaring the pigeons trying to get a drink. Suddenly, one of the female adults in the group glanced in Hardy's direction and her face froze. Excitedly, she grasped one of the men, presumably her husband, and pointed toward Hardy. He searched where she indicated, his eyes darting about, finally resting on, not Hardy, but Fania.

The anger-then-fear overtaking the migrants' faces transfixed Hardy. He glanced at Fania, but she was digging through her large straw bag in search of something and missed the entire scenario. When Hardy looked back at the migrants, they were moving rapidly down the large walking boulevard, encouraging the younger children to keep up. They had soon disappeared in the crowd of Feria-goers.

For a moment Hardy thought he imagined what he had just seen. Two of the migrants had recognized Fania, for whatever reason, and this recognition had induced anger, fear, and the necessity to flee. He looked back at Fania, who had found her lipstick, applied it, and was softly compressing her lips to distribute it evenly over her lips. Not a care in the world.

Hardy wondered what Fania would have done had she seen the same reactions in the migrants he had just witnessed. He wondered if she would have recoiled, seeing that they recognized her. He wondered what Fania's connection was to a group of migrants in Béziers? He was cognizant of the familiar itching in his throat, a harbinger of trouble.

*****

## Chapter Nineteen

Later that evening Hardy and company walked over to the Allées to try the fare offered by the various food tents.  After checking out the Brazilian grilled meats the group decided to go with the fragrant paella stewing in gigantic woks outside Le Cristal with bottles of wine from several local wineries.

Sated, the cyclists wandered down to the area in front of the theater where a large crowd had gathered to enjoy and dance to the music of the pop band, The Gypsy Queens. The feel-good music, much like the Beach Boys or early Beatles, had the crowd rockin' and singing along.  Even kids, in the company of their parents, were dancing and running around.

"The lead singer is drop-dead gorgeous!" Lilith drooled.

Hardy thought she looked a bit liked a venomous spider anticipating a juicy meal.  The thought made him shiver.

Delia let out a shriek.  "Oh, look!" she cried.  "Lane is being propositioned!"

It was true.  A rather dumpy woman who looked at least sixty, sagging in all the wrong places, had Lane cornered and was lewdly flaunting her wares.  Her makeup was cracking, one eye appeared larger than the other because the mascara was unevenly applied, and her thick red lipstick cut a hideous gash on her face.  The effect was sadly comic, and the group stood, amused, while Lane finally managed to extricate himself and escape.

"Did you see that crazy old woman?" he breathlessly asked after rejoining his fellow travelers.

"Quite a handful, Lane, from where I stood," Harold offered.

Delia was laughing so hard tears streamed down her cheeks. "What an absolute hoot! Accosted by a French Madame!"

"Looked like she had been rode hard and put away wet," Fred commented.

"She wanted thirty euros, for Pete's sake! Can you imagine anybody paying ..."

He was interrupted by Fred pointing toward the end of the Jean Jaurès plaza. "They've started the music and light show on the fountain," he said. "I'm heading down for a look.

The lighted fountain drew lots of bystanders as the colorful jets of water surged and splashed to Oldie-Goldies music. Hardy was enjoying the Rolling Stones classic 'Jumpin' Jack Flash' when he spotted some of the migrants he had seen earlier in the day while having coffee with Fania. It was a husband and wife with two children. The children had wormed their way to the front of the crowd where they squealed with delight as the occasional spray of water from the fountain misted over the audience where they stood.

He eased his way through the crowd until he was standing next to the patriarch of the tribe. The gaunt man needed a haircut and a bath, Hardy decided, and moved to the man's opposite side, hoping to be upwind a bit. The man gave Hardy a sharp, short look, and continued to glance nervously about. His dark eyes were the eyes of a living soul who has lost his way and finds himself on a slippery slope in a constantly changing landscape that offers little or no security.

The woman in his company was the same woman who had recognized Fania and sounded the alarm earlier near Le Cristal. She looked to be in her early thirties and was striking in her appearance. Her delicate light skin was flawless, features perfectly blended, her hair a luxurious dark, tangled mass tinged with red, but the strength of her beauty lay in the liberation of her soul that was evidenced by the tilt of her head, slightly defiant lips, her steady gaze, and posture that defined her space and a buffer zone all round.

"Good evening, Madame," Hardy began.

She responded with a slight nod, then looked back to the light display.

"I saw you earlier today, down by the statue," he persisted.

She was instantly wary. A confused look settled on her face; she shook her head, at the same time pulling away from him.

"Please," he said, "I mean you no harm and I think you can help me."

She turned back to him and her husband, Nadim, moved in close.

"What does he want, Hafida?" he growled. "Who is he?"

Buttressed by her husband, Hafida stood, waiting for Hardy's next move.

Hardy saw his chance and took it. "I was sitting with a lady outside Le Cristal and when you saw her you looked frightened ... you pointed her out to your husband and then ran off with your children."

Fear overcame the strong features and Hafida became a hunted animal, wide-eyed, desperate to flee. Her husband grabbed her arm to propel her away through the crowd but Hardy intervened.

"No! Wait! I just need to know ... why do you fear this woman?"

Nadim snarled and spat on the pavement. Hafida wrung her hands, then rubbed them harshly over her rough skirt, all the while shaking her head and muttering.

"Please," Hardy said again, more softly ... pleading.

The decision to run or trust this stranger played out in Hafida's face. Her mind was made up when her children, laughing, ran to her, the youngest girl grabbing her mother's legs and pointing excitedly at the dancing, colored waters. She bent down, smoothing the child's hair, patting her adoring face. The older child, a boy of about seven, looked quizzically at Hardy, sensing his parent's tenseness.

Abruptly, Hafida turned toward the winding concrete ramp that snaked its way up from the Gambetta Quartier, a neighborhood of mixed Arabic cultures, with her children and husband in tow. They would soon be lost in the protective shroud of a blend of civilizations.

Hardy made no attempt to follow. It would be pointless. Hafida's survival instinct was in high gear, her first thought to protect her children. He went, instead to The Drunken Camel, a bar several doors down from his hotel, and nursed a pale lager before heading back to his room for the night. He saw no sign of the man called Chaumont and remembered Alain's admonition to steer clear of the killer.

*****

Chapter Twenty

Hafida often wondered why she and Nadim had left their home in the Rif Mountains in northwestern Morocco. She missed Chefchaouen, the blue pearl of Morocco, where the buildings and walkways were painted in varied beautiful shades of blue and life had been so relaxed and carefree. The goat's cheese she was able to buy locally was flat and without character compared to the delicacy made by the herders around Chefchaouen.

As an artist, Nadim had dreamt of painting enormous murals on buildings and walls throughout France and had persuaded his wife to leave their idyllic life in Morocco to follow his vision in France and beyond. The journey, as migrants, had been difficult and fraught with unexpected problems, not the least of which had been their bad luck running afoul of Manuel Pirón.

Pirón had been infatuated with Hafida and, when she rebuffed his advances, determined to send her to work the streets in Montpellier as punishment. Terrified by the control Pirón had over their lives, Hafida and Nadim had fled from Gilles Fouques' farm north of Béziers in the hope of escaping to the Moroccan community in the large city of Toulouse, but it would be at least a week before the trip could be arranged for them.

In the meantime, the family was given sanctuary in a small apartment above the Souk el Tieta, a large market in Quartier Gambetta, owned by a Moroccan family who had relocated to Southern France. El Tieta was the French version of a souk, a rather sad but sincere effort to recreate the magical ambiance of a true Moroccan souk.

Absent were the artisans and craftsmen who work leather and brass, baskets of aromatic spices, piles of carpets (no two alike), mint tea vendors, hawkers, winding alleys of goods promising mystery, and the magicians and snake charmers. What Souk el Tieta offered was mountains of fresh fruit (especially citrus) and vegetables, a variety of packaged dates, piles of flatbread, honey-soaked sweets, a large assortment of essential kitchenware, and the odd djellaba.

To pay for the temporary apartment Nadim unloaded the truckloads of goods that were delivered to the souk every other day and Hafida ensured that the shelves were organized and full and the entranceway swept and clean. It was little enough to ask for their lodgings and evening meal but ever since Hafida had spotted the flamenco dancer at Le Cristal she had been nervous as a cat waiting for the other shoe to fall in the form of being dragged back into captivity.

The encounter with Hardy reminded Hafida how vulnerable her family was, even in the midst of the heavily populated Feria. That a complete stranger had picked her out of the large gathering watching the fountain on Jean Jaurès, especially at night, sent her scurrying back to the anonymous safety of the blended Arabic neighborhood of Béziers. Even though this area was only one street away from Allées Paul Riquet, the heart of Béziers, Quartier Gambetta was in a different world. One that offered the comfort of relative obscurity.

*****

Chapter Twenty-One

Early Thursday morning before breakfast Hardy took a walk through the Parc des Poètes, with a special detour over to the outdoor amphitheater where the flamenco performance had taken place on Monday evening. He passed the park police as they headed toward the small lake that was home to assorted ducks and two white swans. They gave no notice of him, chatting as they walked. The crime scene tape was still in place, fluttering in the morning breeze.

He went directly to the area in front of the stage, looking under the row of seats where the murder had taken place. It was pointless: the ground had been trampled by an army of feet belonging to gendarmes, the crime scene prosecutor, crime scene photographer and other forensic personnel, plus the EMT's who loaded up Pirón's body for the trip to the morgue.

'This is a waste of time,' Hardy thought. On a hunch he hoisted up on the stage and glanced around the bare wooden floor. He crossed over to the area where the vocalists and guitarist had sat and looked under their chairs. Nothing. He did a quick search on the makeshift stairs down the back of the stage and the ground there, as well. No joy.

Hardy mounted the stairs to the stage to take one last look around. His gaze swept from right to left, and back again, settling on the large potted palm at the right-front of the stage. He crossed rapidly to the plant and, lifting the lower leaves, his finger explored the soil's surface.

His reward was a hard, cold shell casing; it looked smaller than a 9mm, probably a .380mm. He suspected it would match the caliber of the bullet taken from Pirón's body. There was little point in handling the casing with gloves since any fingerprints from the person who had loaded the gun had been destroyed by the trauma of firing the projectile, but he was still careful and used his handkerchief to pick up and wrap the spent shell. He slipped the casing in the pocket of his cargo shorts, looked to see if there was anyone nearby, dropped off the stage, and headed back to the hotel.

The casing itself did not tell him anything about the murderer. It opened up the possibility that the shot could have been fired from the stage. If the shot had been fired from the stage there were only four contestants in the running for murderer: the guitarist, the two elder vocalists, and Fania. Fania was the only one of the four who had been near the front of the stage at the time of the murder, within easy range of the deceased, but Hardy had had his eyes on her the entire performance, and she had not had an opportunity to fire the shot that killed Pirón. He was sure of it.

That left the other three candidates. Both singers had stood near the front of the stage when delivering their solos and could have easily shot Pirón, except neither had brandished a weapon or done anything even remotely threatening toward the audience and besides, the timing was wrong. Their solos had been long finished by the time of the shooting. The guitarist had never left his seat at the back of the stage.

It was possible the bullet casing had been deliberately planted in with the palm, in which case he was glad he had not handled the brass. In the mayhem following the announcement of Pirón's murder at the performance anyone could have casually palmed the spent brass and deposited it in the plant pot and waltzed away completely unnoticed.

If this were the case the list of suspects would also include those sitting in close proximity to the murdered man, though one still had to take into account the angle at which the bullet had been fired. Hardy tried to remember the several times the audience had risen to its feet to applaud Fania's performance. Someone standing near Pirón would have had opportunity to fire off a deadly shot at almost point-blank range, especially someone over five-foot-ten, a height that would have allowed them an advantage over the victim's height.

The game was afoot.

Upon his return to Hotel XIX after his foray in the park Hardy noticed two Police Municipale on bicycles who had stopped a small boy clutching a soccer ball to his chest near the top of the pedestrian ramp that wound down from the Jean Jaurès plaza to the Gambetta Quartier. As Hardy approached, he recognized the young boy as Hafida's son. His blue eyes were wide with fear.

"What's the problem, Officers?" Hardy asked.

One of the cops totally ignored Hardy. The other, with Asian features, replied, "No problem. Just questioning where this young man got his soccer ball."

Without thinking, Hardy blurted out, "I gave it to him, Officer."

Both cops turned to Hardy, surprise and curiosity tinting their faces. It was the Asian who spoke.

"Excuse me … did you say you gave the soccer ball to this young man?"

Hardy nodded, his smile broadening for his role. "Yes, I did. Is that a problem?"

"Can I see some identification, Sir?" the second cop huffed.

Taking his time, Hardy fished his passport out of the pocket of his cargo shorts and handed it over. Fumbling, the policeman opened Hardy's passport to the information page, comparing Hardy to his picture.

"Are you here on business, Mr. Durkin?" the officer inquired.

Hardy nodded. "I have a tour company and brought a group of bicyclists to Béziers for two weeks."

"Where are you staying?"

Hardy pointed over his shoulder. "We're at the Hotel XIX." He paused. "Is there a problem?"

The second cop did not want to let it go. "How do you know this person?" he asked, motioning towards Hafida's son. By this time the Asian cop was ready to move on and said so to his colleague.

Hardy stood his ground. "Is there a problem, Officer?" he repeated. There was an edge to his voice, but he flashed his good-natured smile. He had been pushed enough and the second cop knew it. As a tour operator, if this American complained of harassment by the local cops it would be a demerit in his file. The cop shrugged, respectfully returned Hardy's passport, and the two officers wished Hardy and the boy a good day and rode off.

Hardy turned to the boy. "You are Hafida's son?"

The boy nodded. The fear in his eyes had been driven out by his awe of this muscular stranger who had saved him from some unknown terror. If not for this tall, strong

American he was sure he would have been whisked off to a cell somewhere, never to see his beautiful mother again.

"What is your name?" Hardy asked.

"Hassan," the boy answered.

Hardy nodded. "A good name, Hassan," he said. The boy was, indeed, handsome. "You should probably return to your parents."

Hassan turned to run down the long ramp to the souk. He paused and faced Hardy. "What is your name?" the boy asked.

"I am Hardy," he replied.

"Thank you, Mr. Hardy," Hassan said. Gripping his soccer ball, he ran down the ramp and disappeared into the crowded street below.

*****

## Chapter Twenty-Two

Thursday's itinerary took the cyclists to the medieval village of Minerve, one of France's 'Most Beautiful Villages.' They left an hour earlier than usual and followed the Canal du Midi almost to   Argeliers, before switching to secondary roads.   They passed through the village of Bize-Minervois, home of the olive oil Cooperative L'Oulibo. Banners hung over both ends of the main street announced the Olive Festival which had been held in the village in late July.

"If we have time on the return trip, we'll take a dip in the Cesse River," Hardy told them.  "The Cesse runs right through the village and there's a great little swimming area that is really popular when it's hot if you enjoy river bathing."

"What qualifies a town to be rated a most beautiful village here?" Lilith wanted to know.

"There is an association called 'Les Plus Beaux Villages de France' that is, basically, a tourist promotion for rural villages with less than two thousand inhabitants that have a rich cultural heritage and at least two national heritage sites. Some of them are very remote and have had their population reduced, drastically, by residents fleeing to better job opportunities in the cities. They pay an annual fee to belong to this organization."

"Sounds like a marketing scam," Clive commented.

"It is marketing, agreed, Clive," replied Hardy.  "But not a scam.  Some of the towns have fewer than one hundred people living there so this designation is a way to promote the villages, preserve their uniqueness, and encourage people to visit to experience what life must have been like before France was even France. The increased money brought in by tourism allows these select villages to survive and thrive. Each is special, and definitely worth a visit."

The last hour of the trip was mostly winding uphill between endless vineyards of neatly coiffed vines. Nobody spoke; they pretty much just gritted their teeth and kept going until, cresting the last hill and curve, Minerve lay below, safely nestled between two canyons formed by the Cesse and Brian rivers.

Under the sun, the ancient stone buildings and arched bridge were set amid the exquisite and varied greens of the vines, olive trees, and Italian cypress with the emerald hills as a backdrop. It was stunning. The cyclists left their bike in the parking lot nearest the arched bridge and walked into the village, pausing on the bridge spanning the ravine below.

Hardy pointed to a walkway following the river. "If you follow that path, it circles the outer walls of the village. The point where the two rivers converge is where one hundred-eighty Cathars were burned at the stake during the Albigensian crusade we talked about. There is a large stone dove monument set next to the church commemorating their martyrdom."

"How on earth did this village get captured?" Fred asked. "It seems completely fortified."

"The zealots set up a catapult opposite the village water supply and destroyed it. Without out a source of water the Cathars surrendered. You'll see where the catapult was positioned when you are on the other side of Minerve. Also, you can see the caves and natural bridge when you are on the walk next to the river. This time of year, you can usually explore the caves since the river is so low."

The group hung together until they were down by the river, then split up naturally as some set off to follow the outer walls and others lingered to take pictures or venture into the caves. They met at the car park above the village and, finding places to sit on the rocky area overlooking Minerve, unpacked their lunches and ate while enjoying the idyllic setting before them.

They sauntered back through Minerve on the way to their bikes, giving their lunch time to digest, then struck out for home anticipating a swim in the Cesse River to refresh and cool down. The river proved to be exactly what was needed for their afternoon break.

"Remind me to pack my river shoes the next time, Hardy," Geraldine said, wincing at the rocks bruising her feet.

"Mea culpa," he answered. "River bathing and sore feet go hand in hand."

Harold was rubbing the grit off his feet before putting on his shoes. "They grow lots of olives around here?" he asked, looking at the festival banners.

"The Olives de Lucques, named after the Italian province Lucca, are considered the 'green diamond' or Rolls Royce of olives, Harold, and grown only in the Languedoc-Rousillon in France."

"What's so special about them?" Delia asked. She sat on the cement dam spanning the river, her feet dangling in the water.

"They are large, fleshy, and an incredible shade of green," Hardy explained. "And once cured they taste very buttery … remind me of almonds and avocados."

"Do they make oil out of these Olives de Lucks?" Lane's French was a bit imprecise.

"They do, Lane. Olives for producing oil are left on the tree until they turn almost black, then harvested by hand. It takes eight kilograms of ripe olives to make a liter of oil. Only about two thousand liters are made a year, which is why this particular oil is so expensive, but it's the perfect oil to use on a salad. Very delicate and slightly perfumed. Doesn't overtake the taste of what it dresses."

"Spoken like a true gourmand," Clive commented.

"If you are interested, we can drop by the olive oil cooperative on the way out of town."

"I'd love that," Clive replied.

"Anyone else?" Hardy asked. The nods were unanimous. "Well, then, we'd best be off before they close for the day."

Like a well-behaved horde of locusts, the cyclists fanned out in the shop of the co-op, sampling the various tapenades, olives, and oils on display.

"This dark olive and fig tapenade is fabulous," Delia gushed, snatching up a jar.

"Wait 'til you taste the apricot confiture," Fred said. "It is positively startling!"

"I just ate one of those famous olives," Clive said. "I want to buy a jar to take back to the hotel."

When the group got on the road to return to Béziers the panniers on their bicycles were loaded with a variety of olives, assorted tapenades, rosemary and olive oil crackers, jams, and soaps made with olive oil.

*****

Chapter Twenty-Three

Hardy nearly jumped out of his skin when an arm reached out and gently pulled on his elbow as he rounded the slatted-wood structure housing the elevator to the underground parking garage on the west end of the plaza near his hotel. Hafida had been waiting for him.

"Mr. Hardy," she hissed. "Please, thank you for saving my son yesterday."

"Oh, hey, Hafida," he replied, recovering from his surprise. "No problem. I don't like to see police hassling kids …"

Hafida tried to remain partially hidden by the large palm growing at the back corner of the small building. It was apparent that she had more to tell him.

"You ask me about that woman, that malik aleabid … slave owner," she began.

"Slave owner? Hafida, what are you talking about? She's a flamenco dancer."

The emotions that surged in Hafida's face were violent and transforming. Tears welled in her enormous blue eyes. "Flamenco dancer, hah," she swore, and spat on the pavement. "She and that Pirón trade in human beings," she choked. "He threatened to put me to work on the street. That is why we have run away from the harvest, but it is all her doing."

Hardy was almost too stunned to speak. What this woman was telling him was the absolute last thing he expected to hear. Little wonder she had been afraid when she saw him with Fania.

"Hafida, you don't know? Pirón is dead. He was murdered Monday night at the flamenco performance."

Hafida's hand flew to her mouth, covering it in surprise after a sharp intake of breath that almost ended in a yelp.

"This is true, Mr. Hardy? What you say? Pirón is dead?" So, what Fania had told to Gilles Fouques was the truth. After shock, relief relaxed the tension in her lovely face. Her eyes softened. Hope was returning, but only briefly. "Then she *is* taking over, this wicked woman." Her wariness had returned.

"Taking over what, Hafida?" Hardy asked. "What is going on?" He was having difficulty following   the sketchy information he was being fed. A sudden peal of laughter carried across to where they stood; it was Fania, flirting with an easily flattered Lane near the entrance to their hotel.

When Hafida saw it was Fania she hastily jerked back into the entrance of the elevator shelter. A renewed terror seized the poor woman. Hardy casually backed into the shadows beside her.

"Taking over what, Hafida?" he calmly repeated.

"The migrants. She and Pirón smuggle migrants into Europe. The dancer woman is in charge. Pirón did the dirty work, but it was dirty work she dictated him to do. She would come to the farm with him and sit in the car like she did not want to enter our world out of disgust, but Pirón would always confer with her before making any decision."

"What farm? Near Béziers, Hafida?" Hardy asked.

"Gilles Fouques. We were brought here to harvest his grapes."

"Is Fouqes part of the migrant smuggling?"

Hafida shook her queenly head. "He is just a grape farmer who needs migrants for his vineyards. I am sure he does not know the truth about Pirón and the woman. He seems a decent man.

"She is an evil woman who loves only money. She cares nothing at all about people and the suffering she causes for them. We are simply chattel to her ... animals to be bought and sold." Giving a light touch of farewell to Hardy's elbow Hafida whisked away, blending in with a small group of Feria attendees who had just stepped from the elevator and were heading toward Allées Paul Riquet.

Hardy stood for a moment collecting his thoughts, then headed toward the hotel. Fania had disappeared into the shopping area scattered among the warren of small, narrow stone streets just off the plaza Jean Jaurès.

Involuntarily, he fingered the shell casing in his pants pocket, still wrapped in his handkerchief, that he had picked up in the Parc des Poètes. Fania. Pirón. Trafficking migrants. There was a slight scent of motive wafting over Pirón's death. Always follow the money. His gaze shifted to the network of shopping streets where Fania had disappeared a few minutes ago. That annoying itchy feeling surfaced in his throat again, harbinger of trouble to come.

He was distracted by his cell phone ringing.

"How's the bike tour going?" It was his mother, Lyvia, calling from Frankfurt. He checked himself. No good would come of telling his mother what was happening in Béziers. Much as he wanted to mention Alain's presence, to do so would send alarm bells off with Lyvia: she knew them and their history both so well.

"Seems to be going well," he replied. "Pretty uneventful, so far," he added.

There was a pause on the other end of the conversation, then Lyvia struck.

"I've been reading an online news source for Béziers since that is your base, Hardy," she began.

Hardy experienced a sinking feeling in his stomach. He should have known better than to try and flummox his mom.

"I wouldn't call the discovery of the remains of two soldiers necessarily uneventful. And a murder at a flamenco performance strikes me as a bit over the top, which leads me to wonder why you would neglect to mention either. So, tell me …. Are you in any way involved with either of these incidents, Hardy?"

"Only superficially, Mutte," he assured her. "I attended the flamenco show where the murder took place, but that was pretty much it. Listen, there is a situation I need to look into ... talk to you later?" He rang off hastily, knowing that was not the last he would hear of Pirón's murder from his mother.

*****

## Chapter Twenty-Four

Lilith Parasold sat on a bench near the ice cream kiosk on Jean Jaurès plaza enjoying a double lavender honey cone. She focused on an ongoing scenario she saw unfolding across the narrow street in the mouth of an alleyway next to the Maison Carne restaurant.

A young woman appeared to be propositioning a middle-aged man who wasn't having it. The woman, in her early twenties, seemed malnourished and rather cheaply dressed. Not exactly a candidate to promote a primo sex fantasy. Even more off-putting was her straggly hair that needed a good wash and the hand wringing she couldn't stop as she pled, literally, for a sale.

The man turned in finality and walked off, leaving the distraught woman on the verge of tears.

'How pitiful,' Lilith thought. Her newspaper editor training sent her thoughts wandering, wondering how a person ended up in such a dire, desperate, humiliating position. Her musing was cut short when she saw Fania walking briskly toward the alleyway, determination etched across her face. Lilith jumped up from her park bench, disposed what remained of her ice cream cone, and moved to pursue Fania. Lilith considered the flamenco dancer a woman of taste and wanted her opinion about shopping in Béziers.

Fania had reached the street worker and, to Lilith's surprise, took her meanly by the arm and was propelling the poor wretch up the narrow alley, away from the crowded plaza. Lilith followed, intrigued. Thirty feet up the alleyway Fania stopped suddenly, turning the young woman to face her. Lilith ducked into the entranceway of a boutique, hiding behind the window display but still able to see what was going on a short distance away.

Fania's face was contorted with rage. She said something to the young woman, who hung her head. With her hands on her prisoner's shoulders Fania gave the poor thing a vicious shake. Her voice rose.

"I don't pay you to stand around; I pay you to f---!" she shouted. She fingered the young woman's dress, then ran her hand on her own dress as though wiping off something distasteful. "Your clothes, your hair .... Filthy! You stink! What man will pay for such disgust?"

Suddenly, Fania slapped the prostitute, leaving angry red welts on her cheek. Tears of shame, helplessness, and hatred welled from the young woman's eyes which caused her eye make-up to run, making her even more unsightly. Fania raised her arm to strike again but thought better of it.

"Go!" she commanded, giving her a shove. "Clean yourself. Then get back to work. Remember, every day you owe me."

The dancer turned back in the direction of the plaza and restaurants. Lilith scuttled into the small shop and busied herself looking at purses. After Fania stormed by the boutique Lilith waited a moment before exiting the shop. Fania had reached the plaza thoroughfare and the street worker was nowhere to be seen.

Lilith couldn't reach the hotel fast enough. She intercepted Hardy as he exited the hotel and, in a gush of words, relayed all that she had just seen and heard. It was impossible for Hardy to conceal his surprise.

"Lilith, are you certain about all this?" A sinking feeling told him she was.

"I am a journalist, Hardy," she informed him, miffed by his doubting. "I know exactly what I saw and heard. Fania is running a young, helpless prostitute right here in Béziers."

Their conversation was cut short when Fania appeared, smiles and haughtiness intact. Lilith involuntarily shrank back as the dancer passed them to enter the hotel. Hardy managed what he hoped was a cordial greeting. They both stared at the dancer's back as she made her way through the lobby.

"Well?" Lilith finally asked.

Hardy shook his head. "Lilith, I believe you, but we are not the police. This isn't our affair."

"But surely you have to tell someone in authority, Hardy," she insisted. "That young woman is being trafficked!"

Hardy sighed, way down deep. "You're right, Lilith," he admitted. "Let me think about the best way to handle it. In the meantime, let's just keep this to ourselves, OK?" He turned to head up the street and paused as he added, "And Lilith, do not say anything to Fania about all this; we need to proceed very carefully."

As he walked toward the main promenade, he replayed Lilith's account and overlayed it with what Hafida had told him about Fania and the migrants. It was a sordid business. What shocked him most of all was that such a refined woman as Fania could be involved in something as despicable as human trafficking. He flashed back on Manuel Pirón, and wondered what else she might be involved in.

*****

## Chapter Twenty-Five

Clotiers and Buvain were just passing the Pierre-Paul Riquet statue commanding the Allées Paul Riquet Thursday evening when Alain stopped short.

"I need to run back to the room for my passport, Luc," he said. "You go ahead; I'll see you at La Paillote."

Buvain nodded and headed off toward their Béziers watering hole and chief place for scooping up local gossip. Alain turned and retraced his steps back to the Hotel Mercure.

He was more than alarmed when he saw that his hotel room door was slightly ajar. He knew the door had swung shut and latched when he left just minutes earlier. The reason for the door not closing now, he saw, was a book of matches wedged in the corner of the jam, preventing the door from closing.

Silently, he pressed open the door with his palm. A dark-clad figure, riffling through Clotiers' belongings, sensed Alain's presence and froze. Clotiers took several steps into his room.

"Who are you?" he barked.

The intruder, a man around five-foot-ten, responded by closing the distance between he and Clotiers so quickly Alain had the sensation of a specter moving faster than thought. The first blow that struck Clotiers was slightly deflected by Alain's forearm block, but it still managed to daze him. A follow-through strike to the side of the Legionnaire's face was lessened when he turned his torso, and Clotiers managed a counterstrike to his attacker's solar plexus that brought a sharp grunt from his attacker and backed him up a few paces.

"What are you looking for, Alexandre Chaumont?" Clotiers demanded.

"How do you know my name?" Chaumont demanded.  He was clearly shocked that Clotiers knew his identity.  His handsome face metamorphosed into a darkened, shrouded scowl.

"Or are you here as Pierre Massoud, the assassin?" Clotiers taunted him.

Massoud suddenly rushed Clotiers, pinning him against the wall with a forearm pressuring his thorax.  He head butted the Legionnaire, drawing blood from Clotiers' nose.

"How do you know my name?" Massoud hissed in a deadly tone.

Clotiers right palm shot out, mashing the assassin's nose, forcing his head backward.  Grabbing his attacker's right arm, he propelled Massoud around and with his right hand wrapped around Massoud's face Clotiers pulled and stepped aside, smashing his foe into the wall.

On most men, this move would have allowed Clotiers to finish his opponent with a knee to the head and groin, but Massoud was not most men.  Impervious to the bashing he had just endured, Massoud charged Clotiers, striking both sides of Clotiers' head with a precisely delivered ear clap, sending shock waves down the ear canals.  Stunned and disoriented, the Legionnaire fell back onto the bed.

Massoud pounced, wrapping his right arm completely around Clotiers' head, positioning his semi-clenched left fist under Clotiers' chin, up against his windpipe and applying the pressure from his entire upper torso.  The fit Legionnaire struggled to break free but could not; the choke hold was rendering him unconscious.

"What the hell is going on here!" Hardy boomed, striding into the room in a mad fury.

Massoud let go Clotiers and turned his attention to this new distraction.  Clotiers' head lolled, and Hardy feared he was gone.  While Hardy's attention was momentarily diverted to his friend, Massoud used this advantage to launch an attack on the newcomer.

He lunged for Hardy's throat with both hands, attempting to apply pressure to his windpipe with both thumbs.  Massoud was four inches shorter than his opponent, which gave Hardy an advantage of leverage.  Hardy broke his assailant's grip easily, splitting apart his reach with his forearms, then levying a knee to Massoud's solar plexus, followed by bashing Massoud's head with his knee. Blood ran freely from his damaged nose; he was gasping for breath.

Any other man would have succumbed to this battery, but not Massoud. Escape was now his only option. As he turned to make a run for it, Alain let out a low moan. Much as Hardy wanted to totally mess the guy up, he chose instead to see to his friend. Soaking a washcloth in cold water from the bathroom, he used the compress on Alain's face.

"Alain! Alain, it's me, Hardy! Can you hear me?" Clotiers responded with a small grunt. Hardy dug his phone out of his back pocket, punched in 17, and when the operator answered shouted, "C'est une urgence! Emergency! Hôtel Mercure, Saint-Saëns. Chambre 213. Venir rapidement!"

Buvain became suspicious when Clotiers didn't show up at La Paillote and headed back to their hotel.

"What the …?"

"Luc. Thank God! It was Massoud! He had Alain pinned in a choke. I think I got here in time. I've called for an ambulance."

Buvain stood looking down at his military superior and best friend in all the world, a rush of emotions colliding in him: loyalty, love, dread, anger, hatred. Alain lay half off the bed, his face void of color. He had lost consciousness. His breathing was shallow and thready. His eyes were closed, his lips tinged with blue. With brute strength he lifted Alain as gently as he would a baby and laid him out on the bed, covering him with several blankets to cut down the onset of shock.

Loyalty among the French Foreign Legion runs deep, an important facet of the Legion's fabric. Alain Clotiers had come across Buvain on a mission in the Mideast during Operation Desert Storm. Buvain had exhibited exemplary military competence and leadership ability in an extraction of French nationals and Clotiers had chosen him, Buvain, to become his wingman.

When Alain Clotiers later served in Afghanistan, Buvain had been with him. Buvain had served with Clotiers on rescue operations in Chad, Bosnia, Zaire, and Rwanda. Between kinetic missions, Buvain hunkered down in Calvi, Corsica, where Lieutenant-Colonel Alain Clotiers, of the elite 2nd Foreign Parachute Regiment, led, trained, and disciplined the Legion's finest. And Buvain had been beside him every step of the way, serving, saluting, and seconding.

Clotiers was held in the highest esteem by his men and fellow officers thanks to his finely honed muscular physique, mind-like-a-steel-trap prowess, spotless service record, and the unshakeable core beliefs of God and Country. Now, he lay like a damaged doll and Buvain could do nothing to help him for all the world.

What would have been for Buvain a sob almost escaped the giant man, but he bit it back and said simply, "Mon Colonel." It was a moment of reverence, broken by the arrival of the medical emergency team who bustled in, all business, emotionally indifferent to the stature of the injured man lying on the bed.

Clotiers was immediately lifted onto the stretcher in a supine and neutral position. While two men secured Clotiers onto the stretcher, the third skillfully intubated him and connected him to a bag valve, which one of the other men took over, methodically forcing air into the injured man's lungs. Vital signs were checked and recorded, Hardy gave a brief description of what he knew, and the emergency team wheeled their patient into the hallway. Clotiers looked a bit less stressed now, Hardy saw, but his eyes remained closed.

"What hospital will you take him to?" Hardy asked the lead medic.

"Centre Hospitalier. There is only one," came the reply.

Buvain accompanied the stretcher as far as the elevator. He pulled the medical team leader aside.

"Mind you take the best of care with him," he said, nodding toward his friend.

This comment ruffled the medic's professional pride, and he was on the verge of a deprecating response when he noticed a vein throbbing in the neck of the killing machine before him and thought better of it. He simply nodded and was swallowed up by the elevator.

Hardy met Buvain in the hall outside Alain's room. "We need to talk, Luc," he said.

"Let's head to the hospital; we can talk on the way there. But first, let's jog over to your hotel and see if this guy has already flown the coop."

\*\*\*\*\*

Chapter Twenty-Six

In his room at Hotel XIX, Alexandre Chaumont hastily threw his few belongings into a well-worn leather valise and phoned Claude Duclos. Duclos picked up on the first ring.

"Mission accomplished?" he asked lightly when he saw who was calling.

Not in the mood for banter, Chaumont replied, "We have a problem, Claude. The situation has escalated, and I am going to need some help."

"Escalated how?" Duclos asked.

"I had a run-in with one of the Legionnaires, followed by another with some American who dropped by…. It did not end well. By the way, how did the Legionnaire know my name? Both my names, actually. And now these two guys can identify me."

Duclos squeezed his eyes shut, unnerved by the turn of events. Beads of sweat popped out on his wide forehead. He knew how seriously wrong things could go from here.

"Have you killed anyone?"

"Not yet, but I'm pretty certain the Legionnaire will be hospitalized."

"My God, Alex! Do you have any idea what maiming a Legionnaire could lead to? This is France, not some tinpot goat village in the desert! You can't go …."

"Shut it, Claude! That train has already left the station. What I need from you now is a cover for being in Béziers. I wasn't able to find the film that was found on the dead soldiers, and I can't leave these loose ends."

"What loose ends?"

"Don't play dumb, Claude. I'm not leaving anyone who can finger me. And know this, Claude, if I go down, I'll take you with me, so get it together."

Duclos was suddenly dyspeptic. He knew Chaumont would never take the fall alone. He, Duclos, would be dragged into hell with him. "What kind of cover?" He tried and failed to keep the dread out of his voice.

"A liaison with the local gendarmes. Something to do with investigating the possibility of terrorists. I will send you the bona fides I'm using for the cover, so you have the legitimate info to pass on to the person I am to contact."

Claude thought a moment. "Thierry is tied in with the ...."

"That guy is an idiot," Chaumont interrupted.

"Be that as it may, he is my only contact locally and he knows everyone. He can refer me to the person you need to use."

"Do it."

Immediately after his call to Duclos, Chaumont sent him an email with an attachment which included a passport for one Rémy Agard matching his to-be-updated identity, and a short CV listing his areas of expertise, where he trained, and any influential contacts.

That done, he took his bag of tricks into the bathroom and went to work. When he emerged twelve minutes later his hair and eyebrows were noticeably greyer, and he sported a similarly grey modified Dali moustache. His hair, which had been parted on the side, was now moussed and pulled straight back, giving him the appearance of a receding hair line. With the addition of tortoise-shell glasses he looked to be in his early fifties. Satisfied, he did a cursory cleanup, took a last look around his room, and closed the door behind him.

Chaumont had already checked out and was heading for the underground parking garage when Duclos' call came through.

"The head of the local gendarmes is one Capitaine Henri Broussard. His office is at 14 Boulevard Maréchal Leclerc, and he is expecting you tomorrow morning. You have been assigned as liaison from my office to investigate the illegal migrant community in the area for potential terrorist activity."

"Thanks, Claude; that works," and he rang off.

*****

Alexandre Chaumont had, indeed, already checked out of the XIX.

"Left about ten minutes ago," the clerk informed Hardy. "And no, he left no forwarding address," he added.

"Did he say anything? Like where he might be heading?"

"I actually didn't see him leave," the desk clerk admitted. "He paid in advance; left his key. That's all I know." The clerk hesitated. "One more thing: he arrived in an Aston Martin, a knock-out teal color. I was standing out front when he drove it into the parking garage."

While Buvain distracted the receptionist about places to eat nearby and asking specifically about an eatery two doors down from the hotel Hardy thumbed through the register to locate Chaumont's room number: 306.

"I need to run up to my room for something Luc. Be back in a minute."

Hardy stopped by his room to pick up his privacy card, then bounded up one flight of stairs to the third floor. Room 306 was partially hidden in a small alcove at the end of the hall. It took less than a minute for Hardy to jimmy the lock with the card and unlock Chaumont's door.

Chaumont had left nothing telling in the room. Hardy checked the bathroom, where he found a slight grey smear on one of the towels. Other than that, nothing. They were dealing with a pro.

Buvain was waiting by the door, impatient to get going. When Hardy appeared, he gave him a quizzical look to which Hardy replied, "It seems our quarry has greyed his hair, Luc. Don't know how else he changed his looks. Now that he knows he is blown he will likely go to ground. Or re-invent himself since he has the bonafides and a friend in high places."

*****

Chapter Twenty-Seven

By the time Hardy and Luc arrived at the hospital Clotiers had been treated in the ER and transferred to a private room. His doctor, Louis-Jean Collado, briefed them on Clotiers' status.

"He was extubated and is breathing on his own, with oxygen. At this time, I see no lasting damage to his cervical area or trachea, but we need to keep him under observation for a short while, just in case. Sometimes things show up days later.

"I've given him something for pain and he is wearing an ice collar. Lots of bruising in the throat and neck area, as well as petechiae ..."

"What's that?" Buvain interrupted. "That last thing you said."

"Oh, sorry ... lots of red spotting from burst capillaries. Both eyes are bloodshot, as well." He paused. "He is still semi-conscious, and we won't know until he wakes fully whether he can talk or has difficulty speaking."

"When will that be?" Luc asked.

"No idea, but if I were a betting man ... he should come to in the next twenty-four hours." The doctor excused himself, leaving the two men alone with their fallen friend.

A nurse bustled in, carrying a small tray with a decanter of water and a glass, which she left on the small beside cabinet. She took her patient's pulse, checked the flow of oxygen, made sure the ice pack around his neck was still in place, and departed.

"Luc, I need to make a call," Hardy said, heading for the door. "Be back in a few." Luc nodded, pulled a chair up next to the bed, and sat. He was speechless in the presence of this, his downed comrade.

Out in the hall, Hardy placed his call. "Mutte? It's me. Don't panic, but Alain is in the hospital here in Béziers."

"Alain, Hardy? What is Alain doing in Béziers?" Then she knew. When Hardy and Alain were together it was never by accident. "The two of you are working together, aren't you?" It was an accusation, then she remembered why her son had called.

"Why is Alain in hospital? Is it serious?"

Hardy took a slow, deep breath before replying. "I don't think so, but we won't know for a few days."

"Hardy," she was almost shouting now, "why is he in hospital? What aren't you telling me?"

"Someone was trying to kill him, Mutte, strangling him," he blurted, and too late realized he had made a serious mistake.

Hardy knew what was coming by the cold calm that overtook his mother. "What is the name of the hospital, Hardy?"

"Centre Hospitalier ... Mutte don't ..." but it was too late. His mother had rung off.

Twice before Lyvia had received phone calls telling her a loved one was gone or near death. On those two occasions she had packed a bag, boarded a plane, and flown to Corsica; one time to claim her dead husband, the second to sit by Hardy's hospital bedside until her comatose son had returned to her.

Staying focused on her destination forestalled the angst and tears that so badly wanted to claim her energy and would have incapacitated her. It was not until she was settled in first class on the flight to Montpellier in the South of France the following morning that she allowed herself to think. This time it was Alain. Alain. What, exactly, was this about? He was a friend of her husband and Hardy and, by association, her friend, as well. So why this sense of panic?

"Why, you old fool," she sighed, "you're in love with him."

*****

Chapter Twenty-Eight

Rémy Agard, aka Alexandre Chaumont aka Pierre Massoud, presented himself at the Béziers gendarmerie early Friday morning for the requisite introductions and formalities for his secondment there under the auspices of investigating migrants prone to terrorism on French soil. The arrest of five migrant women in sleepy Béziers four months earlier who were planning an attack in Montpellier had heightened the city's alert level.

Capitaine Henri Broussard sighed inwardly. He hadn't even finished his first cup of coffee. Just his luck a big noise from Paris wanted to drop anchor in his pond to stir things up and make a name for himself. He made a cursory examination of the credentials of one Rémy Agard and, satisfied by what he saw asked, "How can I help you, Agard?"

"I'd like to see any intel you have on migrants with possible terrorist connections or intents, and a list of all migrants from countries on the watch list," he said. "For starters."

Not intimidated by the Paris undercover agent, Broussard summoned his aide and spelled out the request to him and, when the aide departed, said, "My assistant will get that information for you, Agard, if you will accompany him." There was an awkward pause. "Will that be all?"

Agard fought to keep the anger he felt by Broussard's impudence at bay. He was being dismissed. He managed a "Yes, thanks, Capitaine," thought 'Damn provincial!' and followed the aide out the door.

"One last thing, Agard," Broussard said, stopping the assassin in his tracks. "Where are you staying while visiting our lovely town?"

Agard glared at the gendarme. "Why do you ask?"

"Just protocol. Someone from out of town comes to work on our turf we like to know, that's all."

Agard cocked his head, thought a moment. "The Mercure, I think it's called."

Broussard nodded. "I'll make a note of it."

Capitaine Broussard stared pensively at Agard's departing back. 'There's no way you're staying at the Mercure, Agard,' he thought. 'Slippery bastard.'

*****

Pierre Massoud made small talk while waiting for Broussard's aide to come up with the list of migrant suspects in which he really had no interest, at all. He listened to the many conversations going on in the small groups of gendarmes as they settled in for the day's work.

"Did you see the bull gore Miguel Ortega at the corrida yesterday? I've never seen anything like it all the years I've been watching matadors in the ring!"

"The family is already vacationing at Cadaqués, Spain and having a grand time. I'll be joining them this weekend until the end of August."

"Any developments on the murder at the flamenco performance?"

"My sister works at the hospital here in Béziers. She said something about a Legionnaire being brought in last night ...."

This last conversation was the one Massoud had been waiting for, and his ears zeroed in on the desk where it was taking place. As his eyes casually swept the room, they passed over a poor-quality xeroxed picture pinned to a cork board, a picture of Pierre Massoud, not Rémy Agard.

'It is only a matter of time,' he thought. 'That picture has already been sent up command for possible identification.'

"Here you are, Sir," the aide said, presenting the list to Massoud. "Anything else?"

"Ah, no. No, this is what I need. Thank you."

*****

Broussard's phone rang several minutes after Agard's departure. He caught it on the first ring.

"Broussard."

"It's Bernard Bassez, Henri."

Bassez worked with TAJ, France's criminal record police file. TAJ was the collective memory for almost twenty million files and eight million images saved in a data base used by both the National Police and the Gendarmes for tracking and identifying criminal elements in France.'

"One of your officers sent us a picture of a suspect last night and we got the results in this morning. Thought I would call you and give you a head's up on this one."

"How's that, Bernard?" Henri Broussard asked, now curious.

"The subject in question reportedly assaulted one of our Legionnaire officers on your patch last night. Thing is, the guy in question has multiple identities and a shady background. Spent time in the Mideast. Trained as an assassin, it is rumored. Black Ops kinda guy. He also works out of the DGSE ... apparently does favors for the Prime Minister and his crowd."

Broussard was fumbling through the files scattered on his desk, found the one he wanted and opened it. Staring up at him was a grainy photo of a man, fortyish.

"Are you talking about this Pierre Masoud, Bernard?"

"That's the one, Henri. Also goes by the name of Alexandre Chaumont. Man of mystery. Very deadly. Connected. Must be careful with this one."

"He just checked in with me, using the name of Rémy Agard. Supposedly sent down to investigate potential migrant terrorists. His hair is greyer and pulled back from his face. And he's wearing glasses. Looks about ten years older than this photo you were sent."

"What the hell!" Bassez exploded. "You mean he's posing as an undercover cop?" There was a stunned pause. Then, "Broussard, he almost killed that Legionnaire, a Lieutenant-Colonel Clotiers."

"Thanks for the call, Bernard. Send me the info on him. Gotta go."

Broussard rushed into the office area where his gendarmes were prioritizing the day's work. All conversation ceased, abruptly.

"Where's Agard?" he snapped.

His question was met with confusion and blank stares.

"Who, Chef?" someone finally asked.

"Agard! The guy from Paris who was just here."

Broussard's aide spoke up. "He left, Sir."

"When?" Broussard's voice boomed.

"Couldn't be more than two or three minutes," his aide replied.

Broussard ran from the building, scanning the parking lot. The gendarmes under his command, puzzled, followed in disarray, wondering what this was all about. They soon found out.

"Agard is impersonating a cop. He attacked a lieutenant colonel from the Foreign Legion last night. Damn near killed him. Apprehending him is our first priority, as of now. He is highly trained, very dangerous, and knows people in high places, so let's be very careful and go completely by the book on this one."

*****

Information in hand, Massoud made a quick exit from the gendarmerie. He tossed the dossier in a nearby waste receptacle and hurried to his Aston Martin. He needed to be on a flight to the Mideast before an APB was put out on him or he would be stuck in the EU and capture would be inevitable.

The nearest airport was Montpellier, just under an hour's drive from Béziers. He could be on a flight to Istanbul before noon and be lost in the souks of the Grand Bazaar that evening. Bypassing his concierge service, Massoud booked two flights in a never-used identity; the second flight was a decoy to Dubai, and he sped to Montpellier.

At the airport he checked in under his new assumed name, passed through security and once settled at his gate got to work on his phone. The first order of business was transferring funds from his Paris accounts to an unmarked account in Geneva. That done, he placed a call to Claude Duclos' burner phone.

"Duclos." Pause. "Is that you, Alex?"

"No names," came the reply. There was a brief pause, then, "Things have got too hot here, and I'm heading to cooler climes."

Duclos felt the first wave of nausea from fear sweep over him. It took him a moment to find his voice. "What? You're leaving? Did you take care of …"

He was cut short. "No, I did not. Like I said, it's hot here. My picture is being circulated so I'm bailing."

"Alex, you can't! If this comes out our families will be ruined!"

"Not if; when. I'll become my other self in the desert and revert back to my Bedouin life."

Duclos was almost too stunned to speak. The muscles in his throat had contracted and his tongue seemed glued to the roof of his mouth. Alex' handsome face flashed before him, then that of his wife and two sons.

Distantly, he heard Alex terminate the call and he was left, alone, to face a personal disaster that would finish his career and make him a social pariah. Gone would be the status formerly attributed to his family name. Gone the soirées and opera first nights. Gone the perks and privileges of his standing in society.

His wife would leave him, of that he was certain. It had always and only been a marriage of convenience for them both. Without the social trappings his position afforded her she would be gone, taking his boys with her.

The despair that overwhelmed him suddenly turned to anger. Anger at his father for demanding he marry and forsake his one true love, Alexandre. Anger at Alexandre for retreating to some far-off land and not fighting to claim him, Claude, as his mate. And now, anger at Alexandre for abandoning him, again, leaving him to face the calamity of their fathers' nefarious dealings on his own.

Well, he would show them all. Claude Duclos would not be anybody's fall guy. He reached in the top right drawer of his massive 19th century French Renaissance desk, pulled out his revolver, and blew his brains all over the old-growth oak desktop. It was his final 'F@#k you!' to the world.

*****

## Chapter Twenty-Nine

The cab dropped Lyvia at the hospital in Béziers mid-morning on Friday, bags and all, since she had not taken time to find a hotel but gone straight to the hospital to see Alain. Poised on the outside, inside her emotions surged and ebbed. It was the not knowing what to expect.

In Alain's room, Lyvia tucked her bags into an out of the way corner and approached the bed where he lay, still not conscious. His face, normally honed and sculpted, was puffy and there were patches of fading red dots under his eyes and over his right eye lid. The ice bag had fallen away from his throat, revealing ugly dark red streaks and more patches of red spots with blue around the edges. His breathing was steady under the oxygen mask strapped to his face.

Alain looked the part of a fallen warrior. He had always been in command, a leader of men advancing by the sheer power of his intellect and perfect physical conditioning. Lyvia had never seen him vulnerable. To see him thus made her want to sob, but she did not. Instead, she reached out and took his hand, giving it a gentle squeeze and hoping. No squeeze came back, the steady breathing continued. She sighed and settled into a chair she pulled up next to the bed. She had time; she would wait until he came back to her.

"Mutte!"

Lyvia shook her head. She had fallen asleep at her vigil.

"When did you get in?" Hardy asked. He saw her bags placed neatly out of the way. Lyvia rose to receive a loving hug from her youngest son then pushed him back to look him in the eye.

"Now, please explain this," and here she made a nod toward Alain, "to me. And do not sugar coat it," she warned.

Hardy took a deep breath and let it out slowly. Over the next five or so minutes he brought his mom up to speed on the situation and who had tried to kill Alain. When he finished, her face had set in grim determination.

"Well," she finally said. "I am not leaving Béziers until Alain regains consciousness."

"I'll see if I can get you a room at the hotel where I'm staying," he offered. "I'll take your bags to the hotel and send Buvain over to spell you so you can freshen up and have something to eat. My hotel has a breakfast buffet, or there are numerous restaurants nearby."

Lyvia nodded. "Hardy, is this assassin likely to come to the hospital?"

His face darkened at the thought. "I'll speak to the gendarmes, Mutte, and see if they can post a guard at the door." He flashed back to a hospital room in Italy where a hit man from Albania almost succeeded in his mission to kill Hardy and a member of his hiking tour who was checked in as a patient.

"Good idea," his mother agreed, "though Captain Buvain would make mincemeat out of the guy if he showed up."

Hardy's face split into a smile at the thought.

*****

## Chapter Thirty

When Old André turned up at Gilles Fouques' farm around noon on Friday looking like the beat- up old warrior that he was he was met with wariness by Gilles.

"Who are you? Why have you come here?"

It was true that the old man had not been to the Fouques farm for a very long time. In fact, the last time had been on a dark summer's night almost sixty years ago, as he and other French patriots waited for the arrival of two men who had fled Algeria, bringing intel that could change the future of the French Republic.

Gilles had been no more than a toddler that fatal night, so he would not know or remember André, who was a member of the OAS and who had also been anonymously involved in the 1961 putsch against De Gaulle and escaped to tell about it.

The anticipated information coming from Algeria could have given the far-right factions opposing De Gaulle's position on Algerian independence the leverage needed to prevent the giving away of Algeria to the violent and bloodthirsty FLN. The welfare of one million Europeans who had made Algeria their home and tens of thousands of Harkis would be threatened if the FLN gained power in the north African country.

The two men never made it to the farm. When Gaspard Fouques and the other men awaiting the arrival of Devine and DuBlanc heard muffled shots from the direction of the river they expected the worst, and that is what they got.

"Are you Gaspard's son?" Old André asked in reply.

Gilles stiffened in suspicion. "Yes. Who are you?"

Old André's eyes swept around the courtyard, resting on the giant plane tree he'd sat under that night, waiting, so long ago.

"The night them two soldiers was killed by the Orb … I was here," he explained.

Surprise, then fear showed on Gilles' face.

"I know nothing about that," he snapped. "Who are you working for?"

Old André gave a dry, rasping laugh. "I am an old man, son. I work for no one."

"Then why have you come here?" Gilles demanded.

"My name is André, and I've come because ghosts from the past have raised questions, and I have the answers," he replied.

At mention of the old warrior's name Gilles was flooded with memories of the old days, when his father welcomed those of like mind to his farm, sitting into the night, talking, and plotting and hoping. Gilles sat, enthralled, as the old warrior unburdened himself with memories he had kept silent and hidden for decades. As the tale unfolded, Gilles relived the almost-magical presence of his father and the band of men who had secretly joined together as resistants to De Gaulle's Algeria policy.

He listened to a scenario that could have determined a different outcome for France and its many citizens who had shed blood, sweat, and tears to create a home away from home in Algeria. A home that had been sacrificed at the altar of violence, brutality, and betrayal consecrated by the Algerian FLN, the OAS, and the De Gaulle regime. The Pied-Noir and Harki populations had been the losers in the great deception, lives and dreams irrevocably shattered.

"How do you know all this?" Gilles wanted to know, after the old combatant had finally wound down.

"A local man name of Pirón acted as guide for the squad that took out the two soldiers. He melted away into the shadows during the kill or the assassins would have buried him, too. Pirón came here, to your father's farm that night, to warn us. We were also on their kill list, but they didn't know where to find us. Pirón disappeared for a long time after that. Went to Spain."

"So, who was actually responsible for the murders?" Gilles demanded.

"Pirón said the squad was sent from Paris. They were acting on orders from a general in the Ministry of Interior who was close to De Gaulle."

"Pirón, you said? There was a Pirón murdered several days ago in Béziers ..."

"His son," André replied. "Did you know him?"

Gilles nodded. "He brought me migrants to work the vines," he said.

"Why would anyone want him dead?"

Gilles flashed on a perfectly coiffed head sitting haughtily on a slender neck. The flamenco dancer was cold and greedy, but was she a murderer, as well?

"He was also running a trafficking operation," Gilles told him. "A dirty business, and dangerous. The stakes are high, but so is the risk."

"Are your migrants legal?" André asked.

Gilles shoulders slumped and he hung his head. "I never asked," he admitted. "I never wanted to know; I wanted to believe they were." His tired eyes sought the old man's face, lined like a much-folded road map. There was no judgement in the rheumy blue eyes, only a gentle question.

He did know, now. He had known since Fania's visit Wednesday, when she had come to the farm looking for a family of migrants that she thought she owned. How, he asked himself, could people be considered mere chattel in modern-day France? And yet, he apparently had a crew of such indentured migrants picking his grapes. The idea repulsed him.

Worse still, Fania undoubtedly had subjugated migrants working for her into other professions. Bile rose in his throat as he remembered Hafida's fear of being used on the streets. What would have become of Hafida's children? Would Fania have put them to work in a city somewhere begging or stealing for her? It was a monstrous system of enslavement that preyed on desperate people seeking only to better their lives and those of their children.

"Who else knows about this, André?" Gilles asked, returning to the purpose of the old man's visit.

"Just me," he replied. "And now, you." He wiped a large paw over a mouth surrounded by white stubble that needed a razor's touch.

"Why me?" Gilles wanted to know.

"I had to tell somebody," André answered.

"Proof?" Gilles asked.

André shook his head. "Just an old soldier's memory, son."

"What do you want me to do with this memory of yours?" Gilles wanted to know.

The old man's face lit, briefly, into a faded smile. "It could add some spice to the upcoming national elections," he said.

'Indeed, it could,' Gilles thought, wryly. "But I would need some kind of proof, André."

The old man thought a moment. "Write up what I told you as a sort of confession," he suggested, "and I'll sign it. Kinda like an affidavit."

"What about the older Pirón? Can he verify any of your story?"

"He's been dead for years. But the gendarmes in Béziers know he and I had a connection. They found a note he'd written his son when they searched his room at the XIX in Béziers investigating his murder."

The next hour was spent writing up the account of the murder of the two soldiers by the Orb River those many years ago. Gilles called in his wife, and the two of them witnessed the old man's signature and dated the document.

"Find the Legionnaires in Béziers who are investigating this," André told him. "Show them what you have. And tell them I'm heading for Valencia."

Gilles gave the old soldier a ride to Béziers and dropped him at the train station. The old man disappeared through the entrance, never looking back. Next, Gilles made several copies of André's statement. He left one at the Midi Libre news office and another with the mayor's office. The mayor oversaw a monthly publication as a counter view to the liberal Midi Libre. Two copies were sent to publications in Paris, one conservative, one liberal. Finally, he directed the clerk at Hotel Mercure to put a copy in the room slot for Alain Clotiers.

After decades of being ignored or worse, given cheap lip service about the complicit, evil wrongs done the Pied-Noir and Harkis in the Algerian capitulation, perhaps this testimony of Old André's would breathe life into finally spotlighting a dark shame left festering. Gilles fervently hoped this exposition would create a maelstrom of criticism and condemnation toward the ruling party heading into the imminent election.

He wouldn't hold his breath for any kind of monetary reparation. Total exposure and examination of the carnage, physical and spiritual, would suffice, as well as a profound apology to the wronged populations, along with a shameful and very public fall from grace of the elitists who participated in the coverup. Anything less would be a topical dressing when lancing and draining the suppuration was what was required for healing.

That done, he headed over to the office of the Sous-Préfet to speak with Thierry Jean about the migrant situation, telling Thierry his suspicions about the Pirón-Fania operation.

"Have you told the police, Gilles?" he asked.

Gilles physically backed away at the thought of dealing with the cops.

"No, Thierry Jean. I leave that for you to do."

Thierry merely nodded his acquiescence. After Gilles left, he sat a moment savoring this information on the migrants. So, his suspicions had been correct. There was human trafficking going on under his nose. It was intolerable and he had to do something about it.

*****

Chapter Thirty-One

Alain Clotiers was sitting up in his hospital bed just after lunch on Friday when Lyvia arrived after a shower, change of clothes and bite to eat at the XIX. The swelling and discoloration on his face and throat had abated a bit, but his voice was uneven and hoarse and there was a slight wheeze when he spoke.

Buvain sat like the faithful hound he was, his face split into a beaming smile that radiated relief and joy at his friend and master regaining consciousness.

"Luc, you should have called to tell me he was awake," Lyvia chided Buvain.

"No need to fret, Lyvia," Alain croaked. "I just now woke up, and I'm famished!"

The doctor swooped into the room, followed by a nurse whose chignon threatened to spill from underneath the cap perched pertly on her head.

"I am Dr. Collado, the doctor who has been overseeing your care, Mr. Clotiers," he announced. "It's good to see you are awake and with us," he added, conducting a superficial examination of Alain's face, neck, and eyes.

"Are you able to touch your chin to your chest, Mr. Clotiers?" Dr. Collado asked.

Clotiers reached his chin to his chest, wincing in the process.

"Easy does it," Collado cautioned.

All eyes were on the doctor, awaiting his diagnosis, but they were to be disappointed.

"We'll want to keep you in hospital for some tests and observation for a day or so. Now that you are awake, I'll order some lab work done and schedule you for a full neurological assessment. We'll also run a CT scan ..."

"Is all this really necessary, doctor?" Clotiers interrupted. He clearly wanted to be up-and-on-his-way, out of the hospital.

"I'm afraid so ... standard procedure in these cases." He took note of the slight whistling sound his patient made occasionally as he inhaled, then flipped through Clotiers' chart to find his blood oxygen levels, which appeared to be normal.

"Alain, please just let him do what he thinks best," Lyvia interjected, then blushed at her boldness.

"I'm fine, Lyvia, really. Hospitals are fine for the sick but I'm not ...."

"If the doctor thinks you need to stay in the hospital that is what you are going to do. Sir," Buvain said, moving closer to the bed as though to block any escape attempt by his commander.

An awkward silence followed what Clotiers would later refer to as a mutiny against him. The doctor cleared his throat.

"Right. Nurse, let's schedule the labs and CT scan for later today, and see if we can get Dr. Lafitte in tomorrow for a neuro exam." He addressed Clotiers, "If all results are positive, we'll see about discharging you after lunch tomorrow." He then turned to Buvain, "But under no circumstances is he to be running around chasing thugs and playing Cops and Robbers. He needs to take it easy, preferably bedrest. Agreed?"

Clotiers protested, "I can't sit around ..."

"Agreed!" Buvain and Lyvia said in sync.

"As for diet, there are no restrictions. You can eat whatever you like."

Hardy breezed into the room just as the doctor and nurse were leaving. He noted the smug looks on his mom and Luc's face: two people obviously pleased with themselves.

"What gives?" Hardy asked.

"Doctor Collado just issued protocols for Alain," Lyvia said.

"And?" Hardy persisted.

"Lab tests, CAT scan, and a neuro examination and, if all goes well, he can get out of here tomorrow," she replied.

Hardy's face split into a grin. "Great!" To Clotiers, he said, "How are you feeling?"

Alain made a dour face. "Fine as frog fuzz," he intoned.

Lyvia ignored Alain's pique. "What would you like to eat?" she asked.

"Red meat and potatoes! Cold beer, strong coffee, and a flan," came his immediate reply.

She threw him a sweet smile, said, "I'll see what I can do," and bustled out of the room, leaving Hardy and Buvain in charge.

"Well?" Clotiers queried when they were alone.

"I just got a call from Captain Broussard in the local gendarmerie," Hardy began. "It seems Chaumont, posing as one Rémy Agard, showed up at the station early today ostensibly to investigate the migrant population infiltrated by terrorists. Broussard recognized who he was but not before Chaumont got away."

"He'll head for the Mideast," Alain said. "Once he goes native, he will never be found."

"Authorities have put out the usual bulletins and notified all airports and train stations, but Chaumont is no fool. He no doubt has numerous identities and is adept at altering his appearance. A real chameleon."

"What about his contact in Paris?" Buvain asked.

"Another dead end, I'm afraid," Hardy said. "Literally."

"How so?" Alain asked.

"Blew his brains out all over his lovely office in the DGSI, didn't he?"

Buvain grunted. "All nicely wrapped up with a pretty bow." He turned to Clotiers, "At least we no longer have to worry about any more attempts on your life, Alain. Or yours," he said to Hardy. "So, what's next?" Buvain wanted to know.

"Oh, and one other thing," Hardy said, fishing several folded pieces of paper, with a note attached, from his pocket. "This was left at the Hotel Mercure for you, Alain," he said.

Alain read through Old André's testimony, then read it again, more slowly. He handed the document to Buvain, who passed it to Hardy when he had read the contents.

"Gilles Fouques has sent a copy to the press," Alain said, fingering the note. "With the approaching elections, someone is sure to see this as blood in the water and pounce on the story. This coming out now could fracture the Republican party and hand a victory to the far right as well as to the left."

"Strange bedfellows," Buvain commented.

"Indeed," Clotiers agreed.

"Is there anything more we need to do about the dead soldiers, Alain?" Hardy asked.

Clotiers thought a moment, then replied, "Well, it seems our reason for being in Béziers has been fulfilled since we now know who assassinated them and why." He spoke to Buvain, "Luc, you are free to return to Carcassonne or Corsica, or wherever you choose. Me, I think I will stay in Béziers for a few days. When the press gets hold of Old André's testimony, I expect they'll flood into town looking for the old soldier. I'd like to be on hand to add my two cents to the story, as well. The film you recovered from the murdered soldiers will go a long way in confirming his story."

"Do you really think this information will have any effect on the upcoming election?" Hardy asked.

Clotiers smirked. "Hardy, this discovery could result in a tsunami of opposition to the Republican party and completely restructure the political landscape here in France. It is an event that has waited, unaddressed and without justice, for decades, which will demand all the more that the truth win out. It is a day of reckoning long overdue. The underpinning of the ruling elites in France could be seriously damaged and the resulting fallout might finally disinfect and purge French society of their stranglehold on our government."

Lyvia returned bearing an array of food on a hospital tray, the center piece being a steak frites with a side of green pepper sauce that begged to be devoured. Buvain and Hardy excused themselves, leaving Lyvia alone with Alain. She fluffed his pillows, adjusted the height of the bedside table to accommodate his position, and poured a chilled beer into a glass, producing the perfect foaming head.

Alain was suddenly overcome with emotion by her kindness. He grabbed Lyvia's hand and pressed her fingers to his lips. It finally dawned on the seasoned warrior that he loved this woman. When Lyvia finally looked up, he saw tears in her eyes and, at last, knew the truth.

Hardy and Buvain saw the whole thing, standing just outside the open door to the hospital room.

"It's about time!" Buvain muttered under his breath, at the same time wondering how this would all work out in the end for the confirmed bachelor and his right-hand man.

Hardy grinned. "Another reason for Alain to stay in Béziers for a few more days."

*****

Chapter Thirty-Two

Saturday was the last day for the bike tour to ride to a destination before surrendering their bikes to the rental agency in town. They headed for Pézenas, a lovely small town about an hour and half's ride from Béziers, to explore the Saturday morning street market, one of the best- known markets in the Languedoc-Roussillon.

They passed a statue of a bust depicting the French playwright, Molière.

"He spent three summers in Pézenas with his theatre group in the seventeenth century," Hardy explained, "until his patron, the Prince of Conti, became religious and ran Molière out of town for his immoral behavior. The rumor going 'round at the time was that the prince had contracted syphilis from a courtesan and turned to religion for salvation.

"Every June Pézenas hosts the Molière festival, with plays set up all through the town's streets and squares, along with live music, dancing, fencing … quite a celebration."

Hardy steered everyone to the tourist office on the edge of the old part of town.

"The public toilet facilities in Pézenas are deplorable, for the most part, so if you need a restroom use the one here. Unless, of course, you stop in a café.

"For centuries Pézenas has been known as a trading town and is famous for its craft-making. You'll find lots of ateliers, or artisan workshops, as you meander the narrow streets."

When they arrived at the town's main street, Jean Jaurès, the market was in full swing. Vendors had taken over the large, open area with their booths and tables, selling everything you could possibly need or want and then some. The variety of goods and the colorful displays were appealing and overwhelming.

The color and scent spectrum of the artisanal soap display bled into the freshly cut and potted flowers for sale, which culminated in the piles of fresh produce available for purchase, and it all announced an atmosphere of bounty, freshness, health, and lusciousness.

"These hand-woven baskets are gorgeous!" Geraldine gushed, admiring the brightly woven goods stacked on tables and hanging from the spokes of the large umbrella protecting them from the hot sun.

Lilith was taken by an artisan selling purse and handbag creations he had designed in muted, soothing earth tones. Delia was attracted to a display of jewelry. Lane fancied a Panama straw hat, white with a black band. Clive zeroed in on the cheese and charcuterie vendors, sampling where possible.

Hardy led them through an ancient archway that opened into a small plaza and hung a left.

"In the fourteenth century this area was the ghetto where the Jews lived. They had moved here from Spain, Portugal, and Italy, but France expelled them in 1394. The Knights Templar had their headquarters not too far from here, as well. Lots of history in this small town."

"Were the Knights Templar related to the Cathars?" Lane asked.

"Completely different, Lane. The Templars were knights whose purpose was to see people who visited the Holy Lands arrive safely from a trip that was extremely dangerous. Kinda like storm troopers for the crusades. They were men of prayer and men of warfare. Templars took vows of poverty but, ironically, ended up controlling vast sums of money and property. Among other things, they owned the entire island of Malta.

"What happened to them?"

"They became very powerful and wanted to establish their own kingdom ... in the Languedoc, it seems ... and the king of France at the time, Philip the Fair, had them rounded up and killed, many of them burned at the stake. He felt threatened by their influence and power, and desperately needed their wealth to bail his regime out of debt. He and his father had been profligate spenders. He had pulled the same trick earlier with the Lombard bankers and then the Jews, but hadn't killed them, just taken their wealth."

"So, they were all killed off? None survived the slaughter?"

"Well, there were a group of them stationed in Lyon, which was their main base of operations in Europe. Lyon was the financial center of France at the time and, also, the starting point for the crusades heading overland to the Holy Land.

"The old part of Lyon is a maze of hidden passageways and staircases, called traboules, that connect buildings and courtyards on many levels and the Templars, great engineers that they were, used the existing traboules and added to them to create a labyrinth of secret subterranean networks. If you ever saw the movie 'The DaVinci Code' the movie gives you a fair idea of what they were up to.

"Anyway, the Templars in Lyon got word that King Philip was coming for them, so they escaped to Switzerland and set up residence there. Some early Swiss legends talk about knights in white tunics appearing to help oppressed villages in the Valais canton of Switzerland. And, of course, with their financial wizardry is it any wonder that Switzerland is the banking capitol of the world?

Plus, look at the Swiss flag. A white cross on a red background … the templar cross was red on a white background. I've actually met a Swiss citizen who claims to be descended from the Templars."

They meandered through the prepared foods section of the market, enjoying the sights and smells of the enormous steel skillets of paella, stuffed cabbage with chestnuts, a succulent stew, and roasting chickens with potatoes. A refrigerated case held an assortment of Asian foods, and a small street truck advertised an array of empanadas that looked delicious.

The butcher, the baker, the candlestick maker … all available in the Saturday market. And over it all reigned Marianne.

"What's that lady in the statue famous for?" Delia asked.

"Marianne? She isn't a real person," Hardy explained. "Ever since the French Revolution, Marianne has personified the French values of liberty, fraternity, and equality. She shows up everywhere … on money, stamps, wine bottles …."

The group split up then, agreeing to meet back at the tourist office at two o'clock for the ride back to Béziers. The early afternoon sun shone on the façades of the gracious stone buildings, turning them to a warm, glowing honey-gold, and the intricate ironwork on the railings and terraces, laced with flowers and lush greenery, suggested that the town had at one time been quite wealthy.

They arrived back at their hotel with plenty of time to freshen up and get ready for a memorable meal at the Pica Pica tapas restaurant located next to their hotel.

*****

Chapter Thirty-Three

Later that evening Hardy set off on a walkabout through the Gambetta Quartier, enjoying the casual ambience of different north African cultures plus Turks melding harmoniously on the streets and in the many shops.

He had just turned to head up the hill toward the post office when he heard a shriek somewhere ahead, off to his right. He quickened his pace and turned right onto Rue du Coq. The light was fading but he could see what appeared to be a man dragging a woman into a waiting car about a hundred feet away, up the street. The woman was putting up a struggle but would, ultimately, lose the fight.

Hardy took off running toward the vehicle, afraid he wouldn't reach the woman in time. A cat darted across his path, causing him to stumble, hissing in protest at being disturbed by the fracas.

Suddenly, a small boy appeared out of a side alley, soccer ball in hand. Recognizing the plight of the struggling woman he placed the ball at his feet and executed a hefty kick, sending the soccer ball at the assailant's head. It was a direct hit to the forehead, causing the man to stumble and lose his grip on his victim. The soccer ball diversion gave new life to Hardy's rescue and, sensing the danger approaching, the attacker ducked into his car and sped off, abandoning his prey.

Hardy reached the woman, who had collapsed into a heap on the pavement. Hassan stood nearby, having retrieved his precious soccer ball. Hardy reached down and helped the sobbing woman to her feet. Her long, dark hair had come loose from a tight chignon at the nape of her neck. Her dress was torn, and her feet and hands scraped and bleeding.

"Fania!" Hardy exclaimed.

She stood looking like a frazzled doll, dazed and frightened. The attack had stolen her poise. She slumped against Hardy, shuddering and crying. After several moments she pulled back and looked into his face, her eyes blotched from the mascara that had run in rills down the sides of her cheeks, leaving a black trail of watered-down make-up.

Hardy fished a clean bandanna out of the pocket of his pants and proferred it to Fania, who gratefully took it and wiped her face with a scrubbing motion.

"We'd best get you back to the hotel, Fania," he said. "Are you able to walk?"

Finally, the dancer spoke. "You saved my life, Hardy," she said.

"It isn't me you should thank," he demurred. "It was the quick thinking of this young man and the sure aim of his soccer ball that saved you."

He intentionally neglected to mention Hassan's name and hoped Fania would not recognize her savior as the son of the woman she sought to own and exploit. For his part, Hassan stayed in the shadows, mumbling in return when Fania expressed her profound gratitude, and bolting for home right after.

"Who was this man trying to abduct you, Fania?" Hardy questioned as he steadied her during the walk to the hotel.

"I have no idea. None," she replied. Her body shuddered and she gave a long sigh, as though expelling any residual threat. "I was walking along, and he just came out of nowhere."

"Did he say anything?"

"Nothing," she answered. "He grabbed me and started dragging me down the street. That's all I know."

Back at the hotel Fania gained celebrity status as members from the tour group gathered round to offer assurances and condolences. She refused to go to the hospital, asking only for a very stiff drink to calm her nerves. The manager of the XIX produced antiseptic and bandages, and Fania set off for her room to tend to her minor injuries.

"She's lucky you were nearby, Hardy," Fred said.

"Fred's right. Things could have ended very differently," Harold agreed.

"I didn't think Béziers was a dangerous place," Delia said. Clearly, she was spooked by the attack on Fania.

There was a slight lull in the conversation, then Lane asked the million-dollar question. "Do you think the person that murdered her manager wants to kill her, too?"

*****

With pressure from Hardy, who insisted the local police be notified of the previous evening's kidnapping attempt, Fania answered questions impatiently as they were put to her by the authorities. She was back in her old arrogant form, seemingly annoyed at their questioning.

All this changed abruptly when the policewoman asked Fania if she thought the attack was related to Pirón's murder.

"Why, yes, I suppose so. Yes, it is quite possible," she replied, warming to the idea.

From where Hardy stood, it was as though Fania had been thrown a life preserver as she cottoned to the idea that whoever killed her manager was out to get her, too. In fact, she fully embraced the idea.

"That would mean I am a target and still in danger," she announced.

"Let's not rush to judgement, Fania," Hardy cautioned. He was getting a strange vibe from the direction Fania was heading with her comments.

"It makes perfect sense to me, now that I think of it," Fania responded. "Besides, you're not the one with his neck on the line."

"But we don't even know why Pirón was killed, do we?" Hardy appealed to the officers.

The police did not comment on Hardy's question. He could tell they didn't have a clue as to the reason for Pirón's murder or the attack on Fania. They finished their questions, suggested Fania not go about alone, and left.

*****

Chapter Thirty-Four

Monday was to be the last full day of the hiking group's stay in Béziers, so on Sunday Hardy organized a casual walking tour of the small city to off-the-beaten-path venues for anyone in the group so inclined.  Minus Delia and Lilith, who opted for some last-minute shopping in the specialty shops winding through the old town of Béziers, participation was one hundred percent.

The tour group set out for a small church whose gargoyles on its sandstone front were seriously eroded, the Chapelle de Pénitents Bleus, a few winding streets up from their hotel.  On the way, they passed Mr. Box head sporting his usual cardboard box bobbing on his head with a few assorted cans of food, one baguette, and a shirt on a hanger hooked over the back edge of the box, flapping in the breeze as he strutted along.

Fred clapped his hands in appreciation, and Geraldine called out "Bravo!" as they passed by.  Mr. Box Head scowled slightly in reply, executing an agile adjustment to his gait as the box threatened to fall.

Lane looked at Hardy, a question on his face, and all Hardy could say was, "No idea, Lane."

From the church the group struck off for the Basilica of Saint Aphrodise where, reputedly, the saint had lived in a cave long before the basilica had been built and where he had retreated, carrying his head, after his beheading outside the old arena many centuries earlier.

En route to the basilica they passed through a square featuring an ancient olive tree and a building covered with a beautifully detailed fresco featuring Casimir Péret, a one-time mayor of Béziers, who died in prison after resisting the coup by Napoleon III.

Hardy explained:

"A street artist by the name of Patrick Commency and his team of muralists transform façades all over France and beyond using a technique called tromp-l'oeil, which means 'trick of the eye.' He focuses on persons influential to the history of the town where he paints the murals. I think he has done more than a dozen in Béziers, and I'm sure we'll see several more as we meander through town. In fact, you probably noticed the façade l'Arlesienne on the main promenade."

The Saint Aphrodise church had been closed for decades undergoing restoration but this day, luckily, the group found the church open and took a brief tour of the Roman crypt that had once been at street level but was now down a flight of stone steps.

"This hand-carved alter is where the headless saint lay, and those two windows over there, now underground, were where the townspeople would look in to venerate their saint," Hardy explained.

"You mean this basement used to be on the ground floor of the church?" Lane asked. "How is it now below street level?"

"That's the story of civilization, Lane," Harold explained. "Succeeding generations just built on top of what was already there."

Hardy nodded. "There have been all sorts of excavations around Béziers that turn up Roman busts and artifacts. There is a great little museum in town if you have the time and are so inclined."

Hardy led his group back up to the narthex and around behind the altar where the reliquary was located.

"Good heavens!" Geraldine exclaimed, appalled at the extensive collection of human bones kept as sacred relics.

"This is alleged to be cloth from the shroud that Christ was wrapped in," Fred said, pointing to a tattered scrap of material under glass, lock, and key.

"Alleged being the operative word," Clive smirked, ever the cynic.

"Do you believe this stuff, Hardy?" Fred wanted to know.

He thought a moment, then replied, "Well, Fred, I visited a monastery in Ostrog, Montenegro last year and not only did they have a piece of the True Cross of Christ they also had Saint Basil, an uncorrupted saint, in one of the rooms of the monastery with a priest always keeping a prayer vigil at his body. The monastery was carved into the face of a mountain … pretty spectacular …. and the constant parade of pilgrims visiting the holy site was impressive. So, yeah, I think there is veracity in some of these claims."

From the church they headed to the Old Cemetery in the city, about a five-minute walk away.

"French cemeteries have a special characteristic," Hardy said. "I think of them as cities for the dead. The family tombs and chapels are like small houses lined up on streets. Just my take," he added.

The narrow streets of the Old Cemetery were lined with ancient cedar trees and Mediterranean cypress and many of the old tombs were in disarray. Madonnas and angels of every pose and persuasion adorned the final resting place of Béziers' previous citizens.

"Must be because the families of these ratty looking tombs died out and there is no one to keep them up," Lane observed.

"Strange to see pictures of the dead arranged on the tombs," Geraldine remarked. "Looking out at you … kinda creepy."

On the way to the Old Bridge, or Pont Vieux, they stopped for something to eat at a small restaurant within sight of the cathedral, enjoying a light lunch on the terrace.

"Any news from your two friends about the murdered soldiers, Hardy?" Clive wanted to know.

"There have been some developments," he replied vaguely.

"Such as?" Clive pressed.

Hardy realized there was no longer a reason to keep the information secret since it would be in the news shortly, so he told them what he knew, concluding with, "It will be interesting to see how the press handles the revelation."

"Is your friend, Clotiers, going to be OK?" Harold asked.

"Looks like it. He should be out of the hospital tomorrow."

"What about the murder at the flamenco concert?" Lane asked. "Any news on that?"

Hardy shook his head. "I haven't heard anything about Pirón's murder, Lane. I am totally out of the loop on that."

Hardy almost felt a sense of relief at the fact that he was not involved in the circumstances surrounding Pirón's death. For once. With the situation that had brought Alain and Buvain to Béziers cleared up Hardy could now just enjoy being a tour guide operator. The rest of the walking tour was low-key and uneventful, and they were back at the hotel in time to change for their anticipated gastronomic dinner in Béziers.

*****

Chapter Thirty-Five

That evening the bike tour group had chosen to dine at L'Ambassade, a gourmet restaurant near the train station. They decided to include Fania, who was grateful for the invitation. She would have an audience, something her ego needed on a regular basis to stay sated and healthy.

It was a balmy evening, so they chose to walk to the restaurant which was mostly downhill from the hotel.

"We can take cabs back if we are too full to walk," Hardy assured them.

They passed the Parc des Poètes on the sidewalk which ran down its west side. Open tins of cat food and small mounds of kibble had been put out inside the park for the stray cats that lived in the park. Several strays crouched over the food, their fur dull and dirty, their eyes forlorn with an unhealthy glaze.

"What miserable looking creatures," Delia said. "And the smell!"

"Most of them are byproducts of the French going on their annual vacation," Clive commented.

"How so?" Lilith asked.

"They just turn their pets out into the street when they leave for holiday," he explained.

"What? No!" Delia exclaimed. "How cruel!"

"What happens to them?" Geraldine asked.

"The lucky ones get abandoned outside a shelter," Hardy said. "The rest end up trying to survive on the streets. It's pretty ugly, and there are efforts to put a stop to it."

They reached the bottom of the street where it emerged next to an impressive war memorial and turned left. The restaurant, L'Ambassade, was a short distance down on the left.

Fania tried to install herself at the head of the table, but Lilith intercepted her by insisting Hardy take the central seat. Immediately upon the group getting settled at the table the chef appeared, smiling broadly.

"Hardy, mon ami," he said. "I knew it had to be you from the name on the reservation. Such a pleasure to see you again!" The two men embraced, French style.

"This is a surprise, Patrick," Hardy countered. "I had no idea you left Ajaccio for the mainland."

Chef Patrick bowed his head slightly. "Béziers was a chance to do something beautiful with food. My team and I have created an oasis of gastronomy in this town, as you will see this evening." His beaming smile included the entire bike group.

Clive couldn't pass up the opportunity to get the chef's personal recommendation for dinner, and asked, "Chef Patrick, what would you suggest for dinner this evening?"

"Ah," Patrick said, focusing on Clive. "For something truly memorable, the Menu Homard. We prepare every part of the lobster as individual dishes in ways that will amaze you. Five incredible courses, then our cheese collection, which is superb, and dessert."

Clive was nodding enthusiastically. "That sounds superb!"

"If I may, I suggest a bottle of Clairette de Bellegarde, a dry white wine with a floral aroma of honeysuckle and violets. Alternatively, you could try Picpoul de Pinet, a dry fragrant, fruity white."

"I'll have the Clairette," Clive said, decisively.

Patrick motioned for one of the waiters. "Tomàs will take care of you this evening. I must get back to my pots and pans," he winked. "Again, I am honored you are dining with us. Bon appétit!"

It took several minutes for everyone else to decide what to order for dinner. That done, Hardy ordered two bottles of respectable white wines as well as a rosé from Fougères, and the conversation was soon flowing.

"I can't wait to tell Raynor about all the old stuff I've seen," Delia said. "He thinks I need to expand my knowledge so now I can show him I've done that."

"To see the world in a grain of sand …," Clive intoned.

"What's that supposed to mean?" Delia asked, not sure if she should be offended.

"It's just a William Blake quote," Harold explained, trying to cover up Clive's intended slight.

"Who's this William Blake guy?" Delia asked. "Was he an explorer or something?"

"Uh, not quite, dear," Geraldine said, delicately.

"Oh, for pity's sake!" Clive huffed.

Delia did one of her wide-eyed looks in slow motion, then went dark.

"What about you, Hardy?" Fred queried. "Are you heading back to the States after tomorrow?"

"I think I'll hang around for a few days, Fred," he answered. "Spend some time with my mom."

"What about you, Fania?" Lilith asked, innocently. "Do you have anything to keep you in Béziers?"

Hardy threw a quick glance at Lilith, who avoided his gaze. Clearly, she intended to zero in on her prey.

The question caught Fania off guard, but she quickly recouped.

"My bags are packed and waiting by the door," Fania said breezily.

"Oh, really?" Lilith persisted, a bit of a smirk on her face.

Fania was suddenly leery. "Yes, really. Why do you ask?"

"What about you, Lilith?" Hardy broke in, hoping to sever the attack. "Isn't this a picturesque time to be back in Vermont?"

"Quite," she replied. She was piqued at Hardy's interference in her effort to pin Fania, but undeterred. Almost casually she mentioned, "There seem to be an unusual number of migrants in Béziers." Hardy held his breath. "I saw one young woman rather shabbily dressed the other day near the Cristal Café …. She appeared to be offering herself to some man walking by. Her handler was not happy when she lost the sale."

The effect of her words on Fania was arresting. It took a moment for the implication behind Lilith's comment to sink in and the transition in Fania's comportment was chilling. The dancer went from warm superiority to ice-cold haughtiness in one short gasp. Fania's face took on a granite hardness that distorted her features into something frightening.

Ever the obtuse, Lane interjected, "What is going on here?"

He looked from Lilith to Fania, and then to Hardy. Hardy, for once, was at a loss for words. Even Geraldine could offer nothing by way of a conciliatory platitude. Her husband puffed on his pipe with concentration, Clive steadfastly sipped his expensive wine, and Fred fidgeted with his napkin.

The awkwardness was broken by Tomàs stopping by their table to take orders for dessert and coffee, but the tension remained throughout the final course and no amount of Delia's chatter could dispel it. Lilith remained unrepentant for her sustained assault on Fania, wearing an unperturbable smugness that Hardy wanted desperately to shake off her face but could not.

Fania remained cold and aloof, but she had retreated into herself; her exterior shell seemed opaque and impenetrable. She felt no shame, at all, for Lilith's oblique attempt to call her out as a human trafficker, but only a hot anger toward her nemesis and a lesser heat toward the rest of the group now that they had seen her exposed underbelly. Who were they to judge her!

Finally, the grand meal came to an end, the checks settled. The group rose as one, save Fania, to leave. Hardy lagged behind. He would accompany Fania back to the hotel. He felt responsible for Lilith's abhorrent behavior as head of the tour group and would try to make some kind of amends.

Halfway up the block Fania said, "Oh, I forgot my shawl. Hardy, would you mind going back to the restaurant for it?"

He retraced his steps to L'Ambassade and upon reaching the restaurant he spotted Fania's shawl hanging on a hook against the wall. It was the magnificent scarf she had worn during the shawl dance, her final number at the flamenco performance in the Parc des Poètes that fateful night when Pirón was killed.

The shawl billowed out when he did a reverse tug to remove it from the hook where it rested. It was framed by the lighting behind it, blocking it out, except for one tiny hole where the fabric of the shawl was missing.

Curious, Hardy pulled the shawl to him, looking for the small void in the fabric that had been outlined by the light shining through. When at last he found the perfectly round hole he knew, instinctively, what had caused it. This was confirmed when he held the damaged area of the shawl to his nose and smelled the very faint odor of gunpowder.

"Aw, damn," he muttered.

*****

## Chapter Thirty-Six

The cyclists stood outside the Hotel XIX early Monday morning waiting for Fania to be arrested by the police following Hardy's report to them of what he had discovered with her shawl along with the bullet he had retrieved from the potted plant on the stage of the flamenco performance. The cops arrived early and descended on her room in the hotel.

For the first time, ever, in his dealings with criminals Hardy felt a pang of remorse that he was responsible for the flamenco dancer's downfall. He said as much to Lilith, who was standing nearby watching Fania being carted off by the gendarmes.

"No way, Hardy," Lilith argued. "Fania alone is responsible for her undoing. She is a human trafficker for Pete's sake, as well as a murderer. Think of that poor young woman she forced into prostitution … and who knows how many others."

Hafia's regal face flashed through Hardy's mind. Fania had threatened to put her on the street, too, and she had children and a husband.

'Lilith is right,' he thought. 'Fania is a self-centered, greedy, heartless person. And a helluva flamenco dancer.' He let go of the guilt and turned to find his mom watching. She moved to his side and slipped her arm through his.

"Well done, Hardy," she said.

He put his strong, bronzed arm around his mom's shoulders and pulled her close, resting his chin affectionately on top of her head.

"How is Alain?" he asked.

She pulled away enough to look up at her son. "Alain is mending and will be fine, thanks to you." She paused. "And I do thank you, son. These past few days have shown me what I was too stubborn to admit before. If Alain had been killed, I never would have known, so we are both very grateful to you."

"I guess that means you'll be staying on in Béziers a few more days," he teased.

"Just a few," she agreed. "Alain said something about he and Buvain heading for Istanbul … apparently that Masoud villain was spotted there. Buvain is itching to settle a score with the guy."

"Is Alain up for that? Masoud, by all accounts, is a deadly assassin." He felt a prickle of alarm at what could go down in Istanbul, even with Buvain present.

Just then a soccer ball rolled past Hardy's feet with Hassan in pursuit. Hafia was close behind and she was smiling. Her beautiful face was glowing, she was so happy. It was the first time Hardy had ever seen her relaxed, free of her fear of Fania.

Thierry Jean sidled up near where Hardy stood to watch Fania being taken into custody by the gendarmes, an almost gloating smile on his face. Hardy noticed a big, red, goose egg on Thierry's forehead and wondered what he had run in to.

A small, white Peugeot van pulled up in front of the hotel and a delivery man jumped out. From the back of the van, he lifted a stack of Midi Libre newspapers and an armful of the mayor's counterpoint publication, which he deposited at the entrance of the Hotel XIX. Although the two media sources were traditionally opposing in their views the headlines of each were, for once, in sympatico.

"Murder of Soldiers Found in Hérault Traced to De Gaulle Regime", "How Far Up into the Ruling Class Does the Order for Murder Go?", and "Finally! Truth About French Citizens Massacred on the Rue d'Isly." were the headlines blaring from the news. There was an extra vibe on the street in Béziers that Monday morning; the charge was palpable as the citizens buzzed about the information released concerning the assassinations.

In Paris a much grander scene was unfolding. In all the cafés, on the buses and subways, brasseries, and over breakfast tables the people of France were coming to terms, at last, with one of the darkest secrets in the Republic's not-to-distant memory. Among the population's elders it was not a pretty sight as they raised their fists in defiance of the government's obscene shenanigans.

Within hours a protest of thousands, led by students, materialized at Place de la Bastille to denounce France's elites and their manipulation of policies and politics that shaped the lives of French citizens. Chanting slogans against politicians, and Republicans in particular, the great throng headed up the Rue de Rivoli toward the Élysée Palace, growing in alarming numbers as it went. The citizens of Paris had a message for their president, and, by God, he was going to hear it! The National Police were hastily called out to control the swarming masses but soon gave up and joined them. It truly was a new day in France!

Suddenly, Fania and her police escort appeared in the hotel's doorway. Defiant to the end, Fania left the Hotel XIX that morning with her head held high, impeccably dressed, in the company of the two gendarmes who had come to arrest her and take her in for questioning concerning the murder of Manuel Pirón.

The search turned up a small caliber Beretta Pico in the handbag Fania had carried with her to last night's dinner. Odd to think that she had had what was most likely the murder weapon at the farewell gathering. Her magnificent shawl had been bagged as evidence and her room searched for anything pertinent to the murder in question. Her dark eyes were smoldering as she passed Hardy. Her lips trembled as though she would speak to him, but she kept silent.

As Fania was preparing to climb into the gendarme's vehicle three motorcycles, two with double riders and one with only a driver approached on the one-way street, the visors on their helmets darkened and completely covering their faces.

The motorcycles skidded into position around the police car and the two passengers whipped out machine pistols. They fired off several staccato bursts into the air before pointing them at the gendarmes, demanding they release Fania. The gunfire sent the onlookers screaming and running for cover. Caught completely off guard and unable to do otherwise, the police freed their prisoner from her handcuffs and stood as she jumped on behind the lone driver.

The gunmen fired shots into the tires of the police car rendering it undriveable and the motorcycles sped off. The gendarmes hastily radioed their command to report the attack and abduction, then waited for colleagues to come pick them up. A tow truck came for their disabled vehicle.

The bicycle group, who had gathered near the crippled car, were stunned by what they had just witnessed.

"I can't even believe what I just saw," Geraldine said. "It all happened so quickly."

"Who were they, for Pete's sake, and why did they take Fania?" Lane asked.

"Is she in danger?" Fred wanted to know.

Lilith burst out, "No, she's not in any danger! She's a murderer and trafficks human beings. It's outrageous that the bitch got away!"

*****

Chapter Thirty-Seven

Hardy and his tour group's final destination in the Hérault was the medieval village of St-Guilhem-le-Désert, one of France's Most Beautiful Villages, about a fifty minute's drive to the north. Hardy had rented a very comfortable Mercedes Sprinter passenger van for the trip. They packed bathing suits for an anticipated swim in the Hérault River in the Hérault Gorge at Devil's Bridge and left after a quick breakfast.

The drive took them through hills of vines and garrigue, a dense scrubland of aromatic flowers, herbs and trees that influence the terroir of the grapes grown with the same nuances translating to the wines in the region. The Black Mountains loomed in the distance, so called for the beech, fir, spruce, and chestnut trees that give them their dark color.

It was a sunny day in Saint-Guilhem-le-Désert; the flowered window boxes and steps and terraces planted with cascading blooms against the time-worn stone, honey-colored in the sunlight, was picture-perfect. A plaque at the entrance to the village explained that the village was located on the northern leg of the ancient pilgrimage route, the Way of Saint James.

"You will always see a scallop shell symbol on the pilgrim's road," Hardy explained. "This goes back to a legend about Saint James, who was martyred in Jerusalem. His body was being shipped back to Spain since he had spent so much time preaching the Gospel there. The corpse was lost during a storm at sea, but the body washed ashore, unharmed, covered in scallops. At least that's one version for the scallop story."

"Who's this Saint Guilhem guy?" Lane asked.

"William of Gellone was an aristocrat and cousin to Charlamagne and one of Charlamagne's knights who successfully fought the Saracens in the Languedoc and then helped capture Barcelona from the Muslims. He married a Muslim princess who converted to Christianity.

"He retired here as a monk and founded the abbey in 804, gifting the abbey a piece of the True Cross from Jerusalem which Charlamagne had given him. He was canonized in 1066. All in all, a pretty good guy. His remains are in a crypt in the abbey." He paused. "Saint-Guilhem-le-Désert is full of fountains, faucets, and water spigots. Just be sure to check the signs at the individual spigots if the water is potable before you take a drink. Most are.

"The Romanesque architecture of the apse of the abbey is especially beautiful, which is why the village is listed as one of the most beautiful in France. When William, or Guillaume, founded the abbey this valley was uninhabited, which is where the 'desert' comes in in the name: deserted."

The cyclists set out as a group but soon turned into a straggling line as individual interests dictated. Narrow covered passages off the main street beckoned some to climb steps and take a winding back path to the rear of the buildings which eventually ended back at the main road.

A left turn at the mayor's office led to steppingstones in the clear river that ran under the building, disappearing underground. No matter where one walked the sound of running water from the river, splashing from faucets, or tinkling from spigots refreshed the spirit and helped cool the air.

Small specialty shops enticed the travelers as they made their way down the main street. The narrow buildings on each side of the street were joined at intervals by stone archways sprouting vines and plants that had managed a toehold in crevices in the rock.

It seemed to take forever for the group to wend their way to the main square as they leap-frogged from shops selling sausages, honey and jams and olives, an excellent collection of nougat, fragrant soaps, fashion accessories, snacks, and gelato.

When, at last, they emerged on the square, Place de la Liberté, surrounded by more shops, restaurants, the tourist office, and the entrance to the abbey, they took several moments to admire the commercial and social heart of the small town. An enormous, gnarled plane tree, planted in 1855, afforded shade for the stone benches set under its boughs and a fountain invited a quick wash and a drink. An amazing mass of honeysuckle covered several stone arches surrounding the square, giving off its delicious scent and attracting hordes of foraging bees.

"While you all explore, I am going to order an espresso and people watch from the shade of this friendly tree," Hardy told them. He pointed to a restaurant on the corner, Le Logis des Pénitents. "That's where we're having lunch." He checked his watch. "I have eleven-fifteen … let's meet here around twelve-thirty. If some of you want to eat somewhere else, that's OK, but keep the same time frame. We should head to the river for a swim around two."

Geraldine, Harold, and Fred made a stop at the tourist office before moving on to the abbey. Lane tagged along but kept to himself. Delia wandered into an artisanal jewelry shop. Clive made a beeline for a shop featuring terroir specialties and wines from the region. Lilith peeked in several boutiques before settling for one that displayed a variety of crafts and useful items. After examining almost everything in the store she purchased a set of long-handled salad servers carved from olive wood which she stashed in her large canvas bag before heading off for further exploration.

Hardy lounged on one of the ancient stone benches in the plaza, lazily sipping his espresso. The warmth of the day and the distant buzzing of the bees in the honeysuckle acted like a drug on the tired trek leader and his eyelids were soon drooping.

\*\*\*\*\*

## Chapter Thirty-Eight

He was roused by a sudden sharp jab in his side as someone sat next to him.

"What the …?"

The jab came again, harder. "You didn't think I was just going to disappear quietly and forget you betrayed me?" She said it as an accusation.

Fania sat close, leering at him. He was fully awake now.

"Fania! What the hell are you doing?" He tried to move away but was blocked on his other side by a weaselly-looking thug in a black leather jacket, no doubt Fania's motorcycle rescuer from that morning.

Without make-up, her hair disheveled, Fania's elegance had become wanton, her smile cruel.

"I thought we had something," she crooned.

"We had nothing, Fania. We are acquaintances, nothing more," he said, his voice even.

The third jab drew blood.

"Well, acquaintance Hardy, we are going to take a little walk. Just the two of us."

"Where to?" Hardy asked.

She flashed a fake, brilliant smile. "A surprise!"

"How did you find me, anyhow?" he wanted to know.

"Ahhh! I always know where you are, don't I? Are you forgetting? I eat breakfast with your group almost every morning and listen to them prattle on about the day's adventure, so I knew you'd be in St-Guilhem-le-Désert today." She paused. "So, up on your feet, big man. And don't try anything. I'm an adept with a knife."

Fania propelled her quarry toward the street running alongside Le Logis des Pénitents, Chemin du Bout du Monde or Path at the End of the World, which passed by the large parking lot next to the cemetery. She locked her left arm through Hardy's right arm, keeping her right hand, holding the knife, snuggled against his right side. Her sidekick followed closely, then peeled off, heading into the parking lot.

"Just two people out for a walk on a lovely day," she hissed, resting her head on his shoulder briefly.

"At least tell me where you're taking me, Fania."

Hardy forced his body to relax. Fania felt him loosen up and grasped his arm tighter. He forced himself to make light conversation, all the while looking for a means of escape. Hardy felt like he was, indeed, heading to the end of the world.

Just before leaving the village Fania steered Hardy onto a narrow street to the right marked by a hiking sign. It was the trail up to the Giant's Castle, an old ruin that overlooked the village and had once been part of its defenses. It had also, according to legend, been inhabited by a nasty-tempered giant and his magpie accomplice, a bird that spied on the villagers, relaying relevant tidbits of gossip to his lordly overseer. They were a nefarious pair who, also according to the legend, plagued the townspeople until Guilhem took it upon himself, sword in hand, to dispense with the brute, leaving the village in peace.

Fania positioned herself behind Hardy on the narrow path, knife still in hand and quick to jab when he slowed to a pace not to her liking. The sun was at its apex, beating down on the pair with its full August intensity. There was very little breeze to evaporate the sweat generated by their exertions and Hardy's shirt was increasingly darkened by wet patches that clung to his torso.

Fania fairly skipped along, energized by some force foreign to Hardy. She seemed to be in a manic state, one minute humming a catchy tune, the next gabbling on about Hardy ruining her career as a dancer, then suddenly pivoting to an over-reactive observation of the various wildflowers growing on the mountainside.

"I LOVE the scent of thyme," Fania exclaimed, breaking off a piece of the herb and sniffing it deeply and pleasurably. "And the cicadas! Do you hear them, Hardy? Oh, the rosemary and savory … perfume of the garrigue!" She was like a child in a sweet shop, delighting at each new discovery, but it was off-balance, and her behavior unnerved Hardy.

The flowering plants of the mountain scrubland appeared in a variety of colors and design, many of them possessing medicinal properties. The Blue Carnation of Montpellier was a delicate violet-blue star-shaped bloom pleasing to the eye, and there were several wild orchids in a variety of colors and shapes, but it was the proliferation of honeysuckle that scented the air and attracted the bees. The smell had a sedative effect on Hardy, and his energy waned.

His shirt was soaked with blood on his right side where Fania had stabbed him with her knife. Normally a robust trekker, in his present state he felt like he was slogging, mechanically taking one step after another with difficulty. The dry and overwhelming heat was getting to him, and he desperately wanted to quench his thirst, but his water bottle lay on the stone bench under the plane tree in the village square.

"Can we stop for a moment, Fania?" he asked.

"Uh, no, we cannot stop, dear." The ever-present knife gave a slight prick for emphasis.

"I really need a drink of water."

They were rounding a point in the path when the sound of splashing water caught their ears.

"How timely!" Fania said brightly. "I forgot there was a small waterfall we passed. You can water your horse here, but don't try anything stupid. I'm quite good with a knife."

"Yeah," Hardy responded. "I heard you the first time."

Refreshed and restored by the water stop, they picked up the trail once again. The village of St-Guilhem-le-Desert spread out below, nestled along the Verdus River that snaked its way to meet up with the larger Hérault River. They had passed no one on the trail and, looking back the way they had come, Hardy saw no one making the ascent. It was just he and Fania … not a pleasant thought.

He tried, again. "Look, Fania, why are we climbing to this ruin? What is there that is so important?"

"You'll see," she sang out. She was giddy at the thought of it, whatever it was. Her mania made the back of Hardy's throat itch, never a good sign.

On he plodded, willing his legs to move his feet another step. His thoughts started to muddle, his vision to blur, yet Fania pranced behind, driving him on to an outcome he was certain he would not like.

\*\*\*\*\*

Lilith emerged on the Chemin du Bout du Monde from the dark, tunnel-like covered walkway that led down to the gurgling Verdus River, blinking in the brightness of the noonday. As she stepped into the sunlight her eyes roved over the mountain hovering above the village. 'It is all so wild,' she thought. 'How could people have survived such a harsh environment so long ago?'

Her thoughts were interrupted by two figures hiking up the mountain and she wondered at anyone with enough stamina to make that trek in this heat. She cupped her hand over her eyes to cut down on the sun's glare so she could get a better look. Suddenly, apprehension clutched at her gut: there was something about those two figures … something familiar. She fished the mini binoculars out of her bag and trained them on the pair, adjusting to get the clearest view.

'He'll be late for lunch,' she thought, as she recognized Hardy limping in the foreground. "Dear God!" she blurted when she saw that it was Fania bringing up the rear. She broke out into a cold sweat, her gaze frozen on the scene before her. As she watched, Hardy stumbled and fell to one knee. Fania struck out at him with her right hand and the sunlight glinted off something shiny in her hand.

"She's got a knife!" The panic mounted as she realized the danger Hardy was in. "She's going to kill him!" she shouted, and took off, running, to the tourist office. It was the only place she could think of where someone might understand and speak English.

*****

The path to the castle grew steadily steeper as they neared the ruin, approaching from the back side, since the front of the castle plunged down a sheer cliff. Hardy crawled the last twenty feet on his hands and knees, too weak and too unsteady on his feet to feel safe doing anything else. Fania was impatient with this, but at least she didn't menace him with her knife.

Her irritability had switched to intense pleasure as she set foot on what had been the castle's bailey, the open area that was the lifeblood of the castle's activity. It was flat and free of rocks and scree with a thin blanket of ground cover.

What remained of the ancient castle's walls, constructed of the resident golden stone, was found on the back side of the ruin, and consisted of a partial wall with a graceful arched entrance still intact, and not much else. A smattering of wall fragments on the front, that topped the solid-rock cliff, included the remains of the circular keep before a dramatic, deadly plunge down the rock face. It had once been a rather magnificent structure that now was indefensible against the encroachment of the garrigue plants and shrubs that had become resident in the ruin.

Uncharacteristically, Fania helped Hardy settle in a nook from an overhanging wall abutment that afforded a pocket of shade. The trek from the village, under normal conditions, would have been a breeze for Hardy, but in this weakened state it had left him disoriented and in pain. His wound was bleeding again. He was exhausted and the fire of his thirst clawed continuously. His breathing came in short, shallow pants.

"Now, my darling," Fania sang out, "for you, and you alone, my final flamenco performance."

Fania took center stage of one of the cleared areas of the bailey and poised to begin a dance, a cappella. Minus accompanying music, costumes, and the nail-embedded shoes, the performance bordered on bizarre.

Fania began by rhythmically clapping her hands, a tempo then picked up by her feet, but the result was sadly comic. Instead of the driving cadence of the specially designed flamenco footwear she wore during her performances, her hiking boots only sent up clouds of yellow dust.

She glanced at Hardy for his approval and, seeing his eyes closed, went into a rage. She attacked him with her feet, sending thuds into his rib cage and stomach. He tried to shield himself, but toppled onto his side in the process, laying inert in a patch of rosemary.

"Watch me!" she commanded in a shriek, but he did not respond. She grabbed his left arm and pulled him into a sitting position, leaning him against the rock wall. His eyes flickered open. Seeing this, Fania ordered him to stay awake while she danced for him.

Again, she began to dance, following a rhythm that originated from somewhere deep in her soul and spread throughout her body, moving her arms, hands, legs, and torso in a perfection of synchronicity that only comes after years of dedicated study and practice. Every move, every twitch, was dictated by professional poise and mastery of her art, but still, the overall effect was disturbing and off kelter.

Fania's usual peaceful intensity was replaced by a mania that was anything but peaceful. If her aura could have been seen by the naked eye it would have been angry and exacerbated jagged waves and lightning bolts in black and deep violet, pulsing and throbbing like a subwoofer on the verge of cracking.

She glided over the level floor of the castle, now a charging bull, now a matador, a woman of elegant seduction, or a troubadour pining away, his love unrequited. All personas were unleashed to bolder expression as Fania danced the width and breadth of her stage, whirling, pivoting, commanding, conquering the imagination of her art. It was as though she had, at last, been allowed to dance unrestrained by the classic requirements of flamenco.

In a final burst of staccato footwork, her face alight with her newfound freedom, Fania threw her head back with her arms fully extended above her head. This movement, like all others of her performance, was almost violent in its intensity. She lost her balance, something never done, when the ground beneath her feet near the edge of the precipice started to crumble, then gave way.

For a frozen moment Fania did not understand her predicament, the look on her face still sublimely happy. When the sublime turned to terror it was too late. She tried to shift her body toward safety, but there was nothing to purchase.

Out of breath, Lilith made it to the castle floor in time to see Fania plunge over the edge. She rushed to the lip of the sheer drop and grimaced at Fania's body broken on the rocks below. Then, matter-of-factly relieved that Fania no longer posed a threat, she turned her attentions to Hardy who, she could tell, was slipping in and out of consciousness on the verge of shock.

Lilith gave Hardy a few sips of water from the bottle in her fanny pack, then lay him flat, propping his feet atop a stone block that had fallen from the ruin. She peeled off her jacket and her top, covering Hardy with the garments. That done, she called the tourist office in St-Guilhem-le-Desert and told them to send a medical helicopter, pronto. Then she lay next to the supine tour leader, giving as much body warmth as she could.

The local police finally arrived, unsure what was going on. Lilith pointed toward the cliff face, signaling with a downward motion that they should take a look, which they did. The lifeless body of the dancer propelled them into action in an official capacity, which began with trying to question Lilith. Repeating 'no comprendo', 'no comprendo', she finally called the tourist office and asked them to explain the situation to Laurel and Hardy, then returned to Hardy's side.

At the long-awaited 'chukka-chukka' of the medical chopper, Lilith jumped to her feet, waving frantically. Impossible to make a landing on the site of the ruins, the chopper lowered a bright orange medical litter, along with a medic. Hardy was lifted into the plastic basket, secured, lifted into the side of the chopper, and airlifted to University Hospital's emergency department in nearby Montpellier.

*****

Chapter Thirty-Nine

Two days later, his torso wrapped in bandages, Hardy was discharged from the hospital with strong antibiotics and pain killers, and an admonition from his doctor to rest and lay low for a while.  His tour group had left the day before after visiting him in the hospital, vowing to return for another trip the following year.

"One of your tours is like a dinner-mystery theater on steroids," Lane said.  "A live who-dunnit."

"You need to change your advertising strategy," Fred agreed.

"Could introduce a whole new paradigm to tourism," Clive nodded.

"Take the Hardy Durkin Challenge," Lilith threw in, pretending to read the title of a brochure. "Two Weeks of Cycling and Sleuthing."

Lilith's involvement with Hardy's rescue had changed her, profoundly.  Her me-first attitude had shriveled and crawled away, replaced by the realization of how connected we all are in our small window frames of existence.  It was humbling, and she was grateful to have awakened from the self-centeredness that is a miasma to mankind.

*****

"Fania's knife could have nicked the bone," Clotiers explained.  "The doctor wasn't a hundred percent sure there was no infection in your rib cage, so it's critical you finish the whole regimen of the antibiotics.  Bone infections are nothing to ignore."

Hardy, his mom, Alain, and Buvain were enjoying a late afternoon drink at Le Cristal's sidewalk café.  The Feria had ended, the hawkers and vendors packed up and gone, and life on the Allées Paul Riquet had resumed its normal rhythm. The warmth of the late-day sun was a caress on his back. It felt good to be alive and with his favorite people.

"So, Hardy, you have some down time coming up ... where are you off to?" his mother asked.

"I've made arrangements for a trip to the Ionian Islands in a week."

"Greece. That's on the way to Istanbul," Alain commented.

"It is," Hardy agreed.

"Are you staying in Béziers until then?" Lyvia asked. "You could come to Frankfurt for a few days…"

Hardy's phone rang just then.

"Hardee?" a feminine voice beckoned on the other end of the call.

The voice arrested him, transported him to the sunny isle of Corsica. Amelie, a seductive beauty who had an ill-tempered cat with whom he had finally reached a truce, of sorts.

"Oh, hey, Amelie," he said. He tried for nonchalant, but his heart rate had increased, and a light blush of pleasure colored his face.

"Where are you, mon ami?" Amelie asked.

"Uh, the South of France, Amelie. In Béziers. Where are you?"

"Ajaccio, bien sûr." Pause. "Hardee, Absinthe wishes to see you."

'Great,' he thought. Just what he wanted, to see Amelie's spoiled, cantankerous feline.

"And I, also, wish to see you, Hardee. Very much."

"Really?" Her classic French face loomed before him, a vision of innocence and temptation.

"Definitely. And Béziers is not far," she reminded him.

"Uh, well, Amelie … uh, yeah, I can do that. See you tin a few days, OK?" He paused, then added," I'll ring you when I arrive."

He ended the call, a look of devilish pleasure on his face.

"Looks like I'll head to Corsica for a few days."

*****

FINIS